So, he kissed her... nothing even rem...

Her mouth was soft and yielding, warm against his. He felt her hand trembling slightly where it touched his waist, just above his belt, and shivers spread out from that spot and rippled across his skin.

He knew a moment of pure panic, fearing he'd lost track of time and that the kiss had already lasted much longer than it should.

But he did end it, somehow, then whispered, "Bye...call you later, okay?"

She nodded and laughed—an uneven whisper of sound.

Then he was walking away from her, jangled on adrenalin and the alarm going off inside his head. *Back off! Back off!*

He had made what amounted to an unforgiveable mistake—forgetting the Joe Friday mantra: *Just the facts, ma'am.*

Dear Reader,

All authors know, when it comes to characters and plots, that sometimes there are surprises. A relatively minor character can develop a voice and demand his or her own story. Plot twists we never expected can present themselves and give us those wonderful "lightbulb" moments. Oh, we love those moments.

One such moment occurred to me when I was writing the fourth—and what I had assumed would be the last—book in the series THE TAKEN. As Holt Kincaid was explaining to Billie how his parents had disappeared without a trace when he was only five years old, I knew—I just *knew*—I could not leave that mystery unsolved.

Thus began a series of "what if" that grew into a whole new love story I think you will find as compelling to read as it was to write. This is really two love stories, one long past, one present, woven together in a tapestry of love and loss, forgiveness and redemption, of families torn apart and then reunited in the midst of tragedy. Most of all, it is a story about second chances.

Enjoy,

Kathleen Creighton

KATHLEEN CREIGHTON

Memory of Murder

ROMANTIC
SUSPENSE

SILHOUETTE BOOKS

Recycling programs
for this product may
not exist in your area.

ISBN-13: 978-0-373-27677-6

MEMORY OF MURDER

Books by Kathleen Creighton

Silhouette Romantic Suspense

KATHLEEN CREIGHTON

has roots deep in the California soil but has relocated to South Carolina. As a child, she enjoyed listening to old timer's tales, and her fascination with the past only deepened as she grew older. Today, she says she is interested in everything—art, music, gardening, zoology, anthropology and history, but people are at the top of her list. She also has a lifelong passion for writing, and now combines all her loves in romance novels.

For Gary,

My love forever and always.

Prologue

Excerpt from the confession of Alexi K.
FBI Files, Restricted Access, Declassified 2010
I have always known this day would come.

Las Vegas, Nevada

"I was five years old. I remember it because I'd just had my birthday party. My parents took me to a park, and there was a pony." Holt's smile flickered briefly. "I think that was the first and last time I was ever on a horse. Anyway, a couple of days later, my parents left me with a babysitter and went out to dinner and a movie, and never came back."

He said it so matter-of-factly, it was a moment before it registered. Brenna did a little double take, then whispered, "What happened? Was it a car crash?"

His hand continued its idle journey up and down her arm. "Their car was found in the movie theater parking lot. My parents never were. They just…disappeared."

She stared at him, appalled, half disbelieving. "That's… crazy. People don't just…disappear."

"Actually, they do," Holt Kincaid said. "More often than you'd suppose."

Chapter 1

First let me say, I am not a monster. What I did, I did for reasons I thought were very good ones, at the time.
Excerpt from the confession of Alexi K.
FBI Files, Restricted Access,
Declassified 2010

San Diego, California
Three years later

Alan Cameron's day began, as it all too often did, with a body. Three of them, actually. They came that way sometimes, in bunches.

It was now past noon, and one of those cases, that of seventeen-year-old Juan Miguel Alviera—whose badly beaten and bullet-riddled body had been found in an alley between a couple of abandoned cars—had been turned over to the Gang Unit. The other two, Walter and Louise Marchetti—found in their own bed by a concerned neighbor, both victims of single gunshot wounds to the head—had tentatively been ruled a murder-suicide, pending the autopsy results. All that was left of that one was filling out the report, which Alan was going to have to take care of himself, since his partner, Carl Taketa, was currently enjoying the pleasures of Cancún with his new bride, Alicia.

Like most cops, Alan hated paperwork. Making this seem to him like a good time to grab some lunch.

He logged off, indulged in a quick stretch and was reaching for his jacket when he heard a soft throat-clearing followed by a hesitant, "Excuse me—are you Detective Cameron?"

He swiveled in his chair, eyebrows politely raised. "I am."

The woman was standing a short distance away between two unoccupied cubicles, looking as though she'd rather be anywhere else but where she was. Not uncommon, in his experience, for people who came looking to speak to a homicide detective.

"How can I help you?" he asked in the mild but authoritative manner in which cops are expected to address presumably law-abiding members of the public, all the while taking in every detail of the woman's appearance and demeanor.

Tall, slim and fit but not all that young. Late thirties to early forties, probably, and keeps herself in good shape with regular trips to the gym, or maybe the tennis court.

Definitely not physical labor—her manicure's too perfect, skin too good. Obviously uses sunscreen...

Attractive, definitely. Vivid blue eyes fringed with lashes that were thick enough to be suspect but which he was almost certain were real. Elizabeth Taylor eyes, he thought to himself. Straight, glossy dark brown hair in an up-to-date style and cut that had set her back some serious coin. It was only the woman's rather angular features that, in his opinion, kept her from being drop-dead gorgeous. And, also in his opinion, made her infinitely more interesting.

Well-dressed, well-kept, competent-looking—not the sort of person he was used to seeing in his job on a regular basis, for sure.

"I'm not sure," she said, but approached now with steady steps, as if she'd come to a difficult decision. "Are you the person I should speak to about a—I guess you would call it a cold case?"

Alan's pulse kicked up a notch; there wasn't a homicide detective alive who didn't dream of closing a cold case. Hiding his interest behind a polite, "I can help you with that," he swiveled back to his computer and placed his hand on the mouse. "Which case are we talking about?"

She made a small gesture with her hand, and he glanced at her in time to catch the last of an expression as it flitted across those austere features, too quickly for him to read. "No—no, it's none of the ones on your Web site. I did check, but...well, for one thing, your list doesn't go back far enough. This would have been before I was born—in the 60's, probably." She closed her eyes and took a steadying breath. "No, this is...something else."

"Uh-huh." He tilted his chair back and waited. Then straightened up and belatedly added, with a dip of his head toward the chair beside his desk, "Why don't you have a seat, Ms...."

"Merrill. Lindsey Merrill." She took the invitation, but perched on the chair rather than sat in it, shifting her shoulder bag into her lap and clutching it as if she were walking alone on a mean street.

And this time, with his gaze focused on her face, he caught the look of…what? Vexation? Embarrassment? Okay, yeah, but with a touch of fear, too. Maybe. There and then, as before, too quickly gone for him to be certain.

"The thing is," she said on a soft exhalation, "I'm not sure it's any kind of case, cold or otherwise. I'm not even sure it actually happened." Her deep blue gaze slid sideways to meet his, reluctantly, it seemed to him. "I don't want to waste your time."

"You're not." He kept his tone genial, his posture relaxed, hoping to put her at ease, at the same time wondering whether he'd be as patient if she wasn't an attractive, single—he surmised, from the absence of rings on her left hand—classy-looking woman. "Why don't you tell me what makes you think it might be a case, then let me decide if my time's being wasted or not."

"Trust me," she said dryly, "I know exactly what you're going to think. And I *will* say 'I told you so.'"

The little flash of humor was a surprise, and he found himself answering her wry smile with one of his own. "Okay, I guess we'll see, won't we?" He gave her an encouraging nod, and when she still seemed to hesitate, added another gentle nudge. "You say this happened before you were born? So, you must have either heard or read about it. I assume we're talking about a homicide?" She nodded. "Okay, so, let's start with that."

Another hiss of exhaled breath; obviously, this was the

big hurdle for her. She gathered her courage, then: "This is something my mother told me."

"Ah."

"My mother has Alzheimer's."

She waited through about two beats of his silence, then said gently, "See? I told you so."

"Okay." He cleared his throat, straightened and swiveled toward her, frowning. "Let me get this straight. Your mother has Alzheimer's, and yet, something she told you made you think you should talk to a police homicide detective. Must be a pretty compelling story. So, I'm listening."

For a moment, she just looked at him, and he saw a fierce shine of tears come into her eyes. Her hands tightened on the straps of her purse. "It's crazy. It's impossible. I know it is. But…she's *so* upset. She truly believes this happened, and she won't leave it alone. I had to promise her. She made me promise I'd talk to the police. What could I do?"

The anguish in her face was hard to look at. The tear shimmer in those movie-star eyes made him feel slightly dizzy. "I understand," he said, his nod nudging her on.

"She claims—" She cleared her throat, then continued in a choked voice, "My mother claims that my father, Richard Merrill, the man she's been *happily* married to for forty-five years, is not her husband. She claims he *killed* her real husband—murdered him—and tried to kill her as well. Not only that—" her voice rose dangerously "—she says she had another child. A little boy. She says—" she finished it, almost in a whisper "—his name was Jimmy."

And that, Lindsey Merrill, is the part you can't dismiss out of hand.

The thought came to Alan in a flash of the insight that made him—he was not being immodest, it was a fact—good at what he did. Along with the realization that he wasn't going to be able to dismiss it, any more than she could. Not out of hand. Not without looking into it.

His name was Jimmy.

Funny about that one little detail. It changed everything. The rest could easily be chalked up to Alzheimer's paranoia, but not that. Alzheimer's was supposed to be about forgetting things, not remembering.

He definitely wanted to hear more about this, but right now, tense and wired as this woman was, he had a feeling he was going to have to pick and pry every detail out of her. And his stomach was starting to growl.

"Have you eaten?" he asked abruptly.

She looked startled, then dismayed. "Oh—oh, I'm sorry. I should have realized." She popped up off the chair, still clutching her purse. "I won't take—"

"No, no—" He'd already risen, too, and was shrugging into his jacket. "I'm not brushing you off. I do need to eat, though, and I thought, if you haven't had lunch either, we could grab a bite while you tell me your story. We could go to the cafeteria here, but it can be noisy during lunch hour. You like sushi?" He flashed her his most charming smile, hoping again to put her at ease.

Again, without much success. She just looked at him. Opened her mouth, closed it and gave her head a little shake.

"What? Come on, I thought all women liked sushi."

"Oh, I do," she said with the same touch of dry humor he'd glimpsed before, as she obeyed his gesture and preceded him through the maze of cubicles. "I'm just amazed *you* do."

"Don't let the tough-guy image fool you," he said, and was rewarded with a soft laugh. It appeared his plan to get her to relax might be working after all.

As they waited for the elevator, she gave him a measuring look and said, "You're not from here originally, are you?"

He gave her back the look, and was surprised to discover he liked the fact that she was almost tall enough to look him in the eye. That it stimulated him in a way he couldn't quite figure out—and very little stimulated him these days, in *any* way. "Nah," he said, "grew up in Philly. I'd guess you're a native, though, right?"

She nodded. "San Diegan born and raised." She gave a sigh that seemed almost regretful. "I had the perfect childhood. I really did. That's what makes all of this so… *hard*."

The elevator dinged as she said the last word. It had the effect of underlining it, although she hadn't, and in fact, as she finished, her voice had dropped to barely a whisper.

A dozen things sprang into Alan's head, questions he could have asked, remarks he could have made, gentle reminders that Alzheimer's was notorious for robbing people of the best parts of themselves. He didn't say any of them, but waited for her to precede him, then followed her into the elevator.

There were a couple of other people already in the elevator, probably having come from the cafeteria on the seventh floor. The four of them rode down in the kind of awkward silence that seems to be the norm in elevators, most people being unwilling to share even whispered conversations with total strangers. The other couple got off and the silence became even more strained.

What am I doing here? Lindsey thought. *His eyes are so hard…he's not going to believe a word of this.*

Alone in an elevator with a police detective, instead of

feeling safe, Lindsey felt trapped; her thoughts chased each other through her mind like rabbits desperately searching for a hole in the fence.

I should never have come!

But she had, against her better judgment, and now she was stuck. Even though Detective Cameron was probably only being polite about listening to her story, she knew she couldn't just change her mind now and decide she didn't have a case for him after all. He was a homicide cop, and she'd mentioned a possible murder. Of course he was going to insist on hearing the whole awful, miserable story. Then he would say something kind—a little patronizing, no doubt—about it almost certainly being the Alzheimer's talking, and he was truly sorry about her mother, but unless she had something more concrete to give him...

The elevator bumped to a stop and the doors opened onto the street-level lobby.

"There's a sushi place a couple blocks from here," the detective said, once more politely waiting for her to exit ahead of him. He glanced down at her low-heeled sandals. "If you don't mind walking."

"No, not at all," Lindsey said, and was seized by a sense of unreality. None of this was what she'd expected. *He* wasn't what she'd expected, not that she'd ever personally met a homicide detective before, so how would she know what to expect? He seemed nice, and yet, she felt uneasy in his company. He'd be judging her, she was sure of it. She could feel him observing her, scrutinizing her facial expressions and body language. Weighing every word she spoke. Looking for inconsistencies and hidden agendas. Of course she had none, nothing whatsoever to hide, no reason to evade or lie. And yet, she felt tense and uncomfortable.

Maybe, she thought, it's his eyes. *Hard, yes, but not cold. Penetrating…perceptive, too. And weary. They see a lot, those steely blue eyes. And, I think, have seen way too much of death and violence and ugliness already.*

"You're a long way from Philadelphia," she said when they were outside, walking in the seventy-degree early November sunshine, a light breeze from the ocean lifting her hair away from her face. "What on earth brought you to San Diego?" And she knew she was only postponing what was coming, the questions *he* would inevitably ask.

For the moment, at least, he didn't seem to mind. He gave an easygoing chuckle, but when she glanced at him she noticed the laughter didn't reach as far as those eyes.

"The marines, actually."

"Ah. You were stationed at Camp Pendleton?"

"Did some training there." He said it dismissively, and she wondered what kind of training it might have been. He seemed hard enough, tough enough, to make some sort of Special Forces experience seem a reasonable assumption. Then he looked at her and smiled, and the tough-guy image wavered and softened. "Hard to beat the weather. Philly can get ugly in the wintertime."

She smiled back at him, and they walked briskly for a block or so before she asked, "Still…it was your home. Do you miss it? Do you still have family there?"

He shook his head. "No—on both counts." And his face had closed and hardened again, so she didn't ask the follow-up questions that were buzzing around in her mind. *Are you married? Do you have children? Siblings? Are your parents still alive?*

It was none of her business. He was a police homicide detective with a gun on his hip, someone she never would have imagined she would find herself walking and talking with in the normal course of her uneventful life.

So hard to believe, even now, that this was happening.

To *her*—Lindsey Diana Merrill. Once, briefly, she'd been Lindsey Merrill-Hyde, but that had been another lifetime and seemed almost like a dream, now. She was Lindsey Merrill, only child of Richard and Susan Merrill, successful businesswoman, owner of her own insurance agency, competent, content, secure in who she was and where she belonged.

At least she had been, before her stable, secure world had shifted and trembled beneath her feet.

Her mother's face flashed into her mind. Beloved face, with kind green-gold eyes creased at the corners with laughter, and a mouth that smiled more often than not. A face that was only a memory now, supplanted by one she barely recognized, a face with eyes bewildered and shimmering with tears, lips tight with suspicion and fear, lines all drawing downward, making her look…old. That image grew and distorted and became the face of Lindsey's nightmares, and walking beside the ex-marine, ex-special forces homicide cop, she felt helpless and frightened and fragile.

A buddy of Alan's had advised him, in the months following his divorce when he was contemplating getting back in the dating game, never to take a woman to a place where they'd have to eat something messy on the first date. He'd considered it fairly sensible advice, at the time. You'll look like an idiot, he'd been told, and the woman will never forgive you. Among the foods mentioned as first-date no-no's, he seemed to recall, had been spaghetti, tacos…and sushi.

Now, all these years later, he wasn't sure whether he'd grown wiser, more confident, or whether his priorities had changed, but he was finding there was a lot to be learned about a woman from watching the way she handled sushi with a pair of chopsticks.

For one thing, he gathered right off the bat, this woman knew her sushi. She'd ordered with confidence and barely a glance at the menu, and prepped her chopsticks as if she'd been born to do it.

"You like the spicy stuff," he commented, when the waiter had presented them with a bowl of edamame and pots of tea and then departed. "I'm afraid I have to stick with good old boring California rolls."

She smiled as she popped open a pod and scooped the tender soybeans into her mouth, then licked her lips without even a hint of self-consciousness. "I've always liked things hot, even as a kid. My dad is a great cook. King of the backyard barbecue, famous for being heavy on the spices. I probably had most of my taste buds burned off by the time I was six."

Helping himself to a handful of edamame pods, Alan realized he was watching her for the sheer enjoyment of it, and he knew it was time to remember why he'd invited her to lunch in the first place. Time to get down to business.

Her face lights up when she talks about her dad. Definitely daddy's girl.

"Did you and your mom get along?" he asked, and wasn't surprised when her gaze quickly dropped to her hands, busy with another edamame pod, so that the thick black lashes hid her eyes from him.

It was a moment before she said carefully, "I always sensed…I guess you would call it a kind of *reserve* in my mother. It's hard to explain it, but I think I always felt there was a part of her she kept hidden away. A part I wasn't allowed to touch—like the good china, you know? I always tried to be on my best behavior with her—which I think is not true of most kids. Most kids feel secure enough in their mother's unconditional love, they aren't afraid to be themselves, even at their worst."

"But you weren't?"

"No, I wasn't." The lashes flew upward and her eyes met his in what seemed almost like defiance. "But I do know she loved my father. And he adores her—that much I know. I grew up with them. And I've stayed close to them as an adult. I swear to you, my parents love—*loved*—" she choked a little on the word "—each other."

An image flashed into his mind: Two old people with their arms around each other, faces peaceful as they lay together in bed, blood dried matted and brown in their sparse white hair and soaked into the pillowcases beneath... He pushed it back into the darker closet of his mind where he kept all such images, the ones marked *Hazards Of The Job*.

"When did that change?" He kept his voice gentle.

The tension went out of her shoulders and they seemed to droop under the burden of sadness she carried. A burden he thought had become such a habit for her she was barely aware of it now. After a moment, she took a deep breath and pushed the bowl of edamame away.

"When did the Alzheimer's start, you mean?"

Alan poured himself some tea. "If that's when the accusations began."

"No, not the accusations—not then. She'd started showing the signs about two or three years ago. Probably, from what I know now about the disease, she'd been hiding them for quite a while. Until she couldn't anymore. We were pretty sure it was Alzheimer's, and once the doctors had ruled out everything else…" She shrugged and tried to smile, then gave it up as a lost cause. Fiddled with her teacup for a moment. "Then, about six months ago she started behaving strangely. I mean, *really* strangely, even for someone with Alzheimer's."

"In what way?"

"She was…furtive. You know, like a frightened animal. She wouldn't sleep in the same room with Dad—the man she'd been married to for more than forty years. She acted terrified of him." She paused to pour herself some tea, and he saw that her hands shook slightly.

"Poor Dad. He was distraught—as you can imagine. One night he called me because she'd run away. Snuck out in the middle of the night." She threw him an anguished look, then picked up her cup and sipped the steaming liquid. It seemed to soothe her, and after a moment she gave a small, one-shoulder shrug. "He called the police, of course. They found her at the bus station. At the *bus station!* You know what that part of town is like—to even imagine my mother alone in a place like that, at night…" She set the cup down and crossed her arms on the tabletop. "So, I moved her in with me." She smiled at him, and it was both wry and sad. "She's my mom. I didn't know what else to do. Dad was dead-set against it. But we both knew something had to be done. But…" She shrugged and once again reached for her teacup.

"Didn't work out?" Alan prompted.

She shook her head. "She still didn't feel safe. It was okay when I was there with her, but I have to go to work, you know? I'd come home and find her barricaded in the bathroom. Or crouched in a closet, crying." She sipped and swallowed, visibly fighting back her own tears. "Anyway, that's when we started talking about putting her in a care facility."

Alan frowned. "A nursing home? Seems kind of fast. Doesn't Alzheimer's usually progress more slowly than that?"

She nodded. "That's what makes this so strange. According to everything I've read about the disease—and I've read everything I could look up on the Internet, believe me—this sort of paranoia and erratic behavior doesn't normally happen until later stages. And what's even stranger, when we mentioned the idea of moving her into a care facility—it's more of an assisted-living situation, rather than a nursing home, but it's gated and controlled access—instead of being upset, as we'd expected, she actually seemed...relieved."

Alan nodded, then they both waited while the waiter presented the first of their orders, artfully arranged on lacquered trays.

He watched, fascinated, as Lindsey poured soy sauce into the shallow bowl provided for the purpose, plucked up a glob of green wasabi paste with her chopsticks and stirred it into the sauce, then deftly selected a round of spicy tuna roll, dunked it into the sauce and popped it into her mouth. Whole.

She gave a happy little gasp and made fanning motions with her hand while her eyes watered, and when her mouth was free again, said, "Whoo. I always love that first hit. Really clears your sinuses."

A peculiar lightness bubbled up through his chest, and he found himself smiling back at her. "You make it sound like taking drugs."

Her eyes widened and a hint of a flush warmed her

cheeks. "What? Oh—God, no. That never—I mean, I've never—"

"Never?" he teased her, as he doctored his own soy sauce, with a much smaller—wimpier?—dab of wasabi. "Not even when you were a kid?"

"Never, I swear. I told you—I had an idyllic childhood. I had perfect parents. I was the perfect child. It never occurred to me to take drugs—it would have broken my parents' hearts, for one thing. And for another, why on earth would I want to?" Almost angrily, she plucked up another round of spicy tuna and swirled it in the sauce. "I was *happy.*"

"Lucky girl," Alan said, and earned himself a brief, startled glance.

"Yes," she said softly. "I was." The slice of sushi roll went into her mouth and her eyes teared up—from the wasabi, he wondered, or something else?

"You're not married?" He nodded toward the hand wielding the chopsticks—she was a lefty, he realized—as he attempted to capture a sushi morsel with his own awkwardly skewed chopsticks.

"Hmm…no, like this," she said, laying down her chopsticks and placing her hands on his.

Her fingers felt cool and sure and smooth as silk on the backs of his, and he felt a curious sizzle under his skin that rode in waves through his arms and into his chest. A purely physical response to a woman's touch, and one he couldn't recall ever feeling before. Or, if he had, it had been so long ago he'd forgotten what the sensation felt like.

When she had his chopsticks placed correctly and to her satisfaction, she picked up her own and demonstrated the proper way to pinch the tips together. "See? Like this."

He copied her dutifully, wondering whether she was

using the teaching moment to evade his question and whether or not she'd answer it. And whether she'd felt the same jolt he'd felt when she touched him.

"Sorry, none of my business," he said as he concentrated on picking up a segment of California roll. When he had it captured and reasonably secure, he glanced up at her and smiled in what he hoped was a winning way. "Just wondering, because of your name, and the fact that you don't wear a ring. I'm a police detective—comes with the territory."

A hint of an answering smile tugged at the corners of her mouth. "Divorced—took back my maiden name. You?"

He chewed, swallowed, nodded...thinking he wasn't getting that horseradish "hit" she'd mentioned, and maybe he'd try adding a bit more wasabi next time. "Divorced. Kids?"

And the lashes came down—lights out. Okay, so that was a tender spot, obviously. Although her voice sounded completely normal when she said, "No. You?"

"One daughter. Chelsea. She'll be ten in January. Lives with her mother. And is growing up way too fast. I get her every other weekend, unless the job interferes."

She gave him her eyes again, smiled, nodded in sympathy. "That must be tough."

The waiter brought another round of sushi and they talked casually as they ate it, talked of things like his daughter's school and sports and the Internet, the pitfalls of parenting, and why it was a job made tougher by the fact that he was a cop. Being unable to commiserate from the parent's point of view, Lindsey offered insights on Chelsea's, the ways they were alike—as only children—and the ways they weren't—Chelsea's parents being divorced.

"But we're close, Chelse and me—although she's decided

she wants to be called CeeCee, lately. I mean, what's that? I don't even know how it's supposed to be spelled! Initials? Like the Spanish for 'yes yes'? Come on! But…yeah, we have a pretty good thing going—so far. Knock wood."

Lindsey had been smiling, laughing with him. Now, she pushed the platters with the few remaining slices of sushi away from her and leaned forward, forearms on the tabletop, eyes bright and fierce.

"Okay, now imagine it's twenty or thirty years from now, after you've cheered at Chelsea's graduations, danced with her at her wedding, held her and let her cry until your shirt was soaked when her baby died, and again when her marriage ended. After you've given her the money to start up her business and you wouldn't take a dime when she wanted to pay you back. Imagine her mom suddenly out of the blue one day telling Chelsea you're not her father, that you're a monster and a murderer. *Imagine how she'd feel.*"

Chapter 2

They did not try to run or fight back when I took them. They seemed more bewildered than afraid. They said I had made a mistake. Of course, I did not believe them.
Excerpt from the confession of Alexi K.
FBI Files, Restricted Access,
Declassified 2010

Lindsey knew she sounded pathetic, and didn't care.

She thought it probably didn't matter anyway, doubted even tears would make any difference in whether this life-hardened police detective believed her or not. Oh, he was a good listener, and seemed friendly enough—kind...even charming. The blue eyes reflected sympathy at times, speculation at others. And at others, something else, something she couldn't even put a name to. But the key word, she realized, was *reflected*. Eyes, she'd heard, were supposed to be the windows of the soul, but his reminded her of windows in a dark house, mirrors that revealed nothing of what was inside.

"It must be upsetting," he murmured, his eyes resting on her now with what looked like genuine compassion. "Alzheimer's—"

"If I thought it was just the Alzheimer's, I wouldn't be sitting here," she said, and was unable to keep an edge out of her voice.

His eyebrows rose. "So, you think there's something to it? That your father—"

"No! Of course not." That was twice she'd interrupted him. What was the matter with her? That was something she would normally be too polite to do, too well-schooled in effective ways of selling, whether an insurance policy, or herself. Reminding herself that she had a selling job to do right now, she took a breath and started again, this time in a calm, measured tone.

"I'm sorry. But…no, Detective Cameron—"

"Alan."

Thrown off guard by *his* interruption, she caught another breath, a reflexive breath. "*Alan*—obviously, I don't think my father killed anyone. The idea is insane. But I do think *something* must have happened to my mother, probably some time in her far distant past. Something terrible. It's just—you'd have to be there, hear her yourself, the way she talks. It's too vivid, too real to her. I can't believe it didn't come from *somewhere*."

He shifted in his seat to allow the waiter to collect the sushi trays, then nodded, encouraging her to go on.

"What I'm wondering is…" She waited until the waiter had gone away, then leaned toward him eagerly. "Suppose she's been suppressing these memories all these years, the way victims of abuse do. You know? Then, as the connections in her brain begin to fail, the walls protecting her from the memories begin to break down. But the memories are confusing, and she…"

"You're thinking she's mixing up your father with someone else?"

"Yes." She said it on a hiss of exhaled breath, and the easing inside her chest made her feel almost giddy. He was frowning but his eyes were sharp, focused on her now with interest that looked real rather than merely polite.

"And this…*thing* that happened to your mother, it would have to have been…"

"Before she met my dad. So, probably forty-some years ago, maybe? Anyway, a *long* time."

"And you think it happened here—in San Diego?"

She held up her hands, a gesture of the helplessness she felt. "I have no idea. I just assumed she'd always lived here, but now…" She gave a small precarious laugh.

"Has she given you any details? Anything that might help to narrow it down to a time and place?"

She shook her head. "Whenever she starts talking to me about it, she just cries. And begs me to tell the police." Overwhelming sadness forced her to smile. "So, now I have. Maybe you can get more out of her. It's what you do, isn't it?"

The arrival of the waiter with the check saved him from having to answer what was, after all, a rhetorical question.

Obeying protocol, the waiter presented the plastic-bound folder containing their bill to Alan, the male of the party. Lindsey reached to intercept it, and there was a brief comedic moment when it appeared a three-way tug-of-war might ensue.

"I invited you, remember?" Alan said, smiling at her over the contested prize.

Lindsey countered with a smile of her own and, "Yes, but I own my own business. I need the tax deduction."

"Ah, but if I let you pay for my lunch, it could be construed as bribing a police officer."

Lindsey laughed and yielded. "Okay, that trumps me. You win."

He took out his wallet, selected some bills and placed them on top of the folder without looking at what was inside, nodded at the hovering waiter, then rose. Lindsey hurriedly snatched up her purse and did the same, and Alan took her elbow and said, "How's your afternoon?"

She hesitated, thrown off guard in much the same way she had been when he'd asked if she liked sushi, and again when he'd ordered her to use his first name. She was a naturally reserved person and tended to be cautious—even timid—when getting acquainted with strangers, thoroughly testing and getting comfortable with the unknown waters before taking the next step. The detective's abrupt—even snap—decisions were unsettling to her. "I took it off," she said, recovering. "But you don't mean you—"

"Why not? One thing's for sure, after forty-some-odd years, this case isn't going to get any fresher." Alan was thinking about the reports he was supposed to be filling out, waiting for him back at his desk. He smiled into the amazing black-fringed eyes so nearly on a level with his own. "So, let's go talk to your mom, shall we?"

They went in separate cars—her choice, not his, but as he followed Lindsey Merrill's classy silver-blue Mercedes through the streets of San Diego, he had some time to think about what he might be getting himself into.

As far as this "cold case" went, probably nothing. He was pretty sure it was going to turn out to be exactly what it looked like—a case of Alzheimer's taking a peculiar turn, a sad story but hardly one that warranted the time and energy of the San Diego Police Department. And he was going to have to explain to his captain why he'd spent the afternoon chasing wild geese when there were open cases he should be working.

So, why was he doing this? Sure, Lindsey Merrill was attractive, but he was long past the age when his hormones were able to override his good sense. The last time that had happened he'd been about seventeen, and he figured he still had a way to go before he'd reach the age where a desire to recapture those randy days of youth might lead him down those old dangerous paths.

What it was, he realized, was that he'd reached an age where he was beginning to question the paths he'd already chosen. Questioning how much longer he was going to be able to deal with the constant parade of teenaged-gang-violence victims and domestic violence cases—those were the worst, particularly the ones involving kids—without burning out. He'd seen it happen to guys he'd come up through the ranks with. He didn't like to dwell on those stories of breakdowns and suicides, and even now pushed them out to the fringes of his consciousness and tethered them there with the mantra, *That's not gonna happen to me, won't happen to me.*

At the same time, he felt twinges in his side where the knife wound he'd received during a recent domestic violence case hadn't completely healed yet. He'd shot and killed the guy, a righteous shoot if there ever was one, and had just come off administrative leave due to officer-involved shooting—his first—and the mandatory visits with the department shrink, who had suggested he might benefit from some mild antidepressants. Which he'd refused, of course. He didn't need pills. What he needed was to see some evidence that his efforts—and those of his brother and sister officers—were having some effect in keeping the whole damn world from going to hell in a handbasket.

Would this wild-goose chase he was on do the trick? Probably not, he thought, but it couldn't hurt, either. He'd hear what Susan Merrill had to say—if she was coherent— and what was the worst that could happen? He'd conclude it was the Alzheimer's talking, and he'd have had lunch and spent an interesting afternoon in the company of an attractive woman. A very *nice*, very *classy*, attractive woman.

He felt a little smug about the fact that the word "sexy" hadn't even entered his head.

Until now.

Driving sedately and self-consciously, keeping one eye on the detective's anonymous dark sedan in her rearview mirror, Lindsey still had plenty of time to wonder, for the umpteenth time, whether she was doing the right thing. She was honest enough with herself to know that, right or wrong, she was doing this more for herself than her mother. As painful as it was to see her mother so fragile and frightened, what she hated more was the feeling that her own world was spiraling out of her control. Again.

Trent had once accused her of being a control freak. It had been during one of the counseling sessions she'd agreed to attend with him in the weeks leading up to her decision to divorce him, once and for all. She remembered the counselor regarding her in that *way* he had, fingers steepled in front of his chin, eyebrows raised, and asking her what she thought of that. What she thought, of course, was that Trent was wrong, that she didn't see how wanting to have some degree of control over one's own life made one a control freak. It seemed to her that a control freak was someone who wanted to control *other* people's lives.

Lindsey had no desire to control anyone else's life. Just her own. She had no problem taking responsibility for her own bad choices—marrying Trent had probably been one of those—but she couldn't stand it when things happened to her that she had absolutely no say in.

It had not been her choice to have a miscarriage.

Miscarriage—what kind of word was that? It sounded as if she'd made some sort of minor error, dropped something, or stumbled over something. She'd done nothing of the sort, she'd done nothing wrong. There had been absolutely nothing she could have done to prevent her baby from being born too early, so early she couldn't possibly survive. That was the hard truth of it, no matter what euphemism they used: Her child had died. And there had been nothing she could do to save her.

No, she'd been unable to do anything about that, but she had been able to keep it from ever happening again. The doctors had told her the odds were she would never be able to carry a child to full term. Rather than take the chance of enduring that kind of loss and pain again, she'd made the decision that had eventually destroyed her marriage. Trent had been furious with her—had tried to bully her into changing her mind. *But it's my body,* she'd told him, heartbroken that he'd seemed incapable of understanding how she felt. *It's my choice.* And that was when he'd accused her of being a control freak.

Why was she thinking about this now? Surely not

because Detective Cameron had mentioned his daughter, who was almost ten, which happened to be the age her daughter would have been, if she'd lived. No, not because of that. *It's been ten years...it can't be that. Surely not after so long...*

More likely, it was this thing with her mother, watching her change right before her eyes and being unable to stop the slow inevitable slide that was taking her further and further away...seeing the terrible toll it was taking on her father and being unable to do anything to help him. All this was making her feel powerless all over again. Going to the police with her mother's story was at least doing *something*. Taking action. *Taking control.*

Even if nothing came of it, even if Detective Cameron decided it was just the Alzheimer's playing tricks with her mother's mind, she told herself, at least she'd done that—taken control.

Then, in her mind she saw those eyes, Alan Cameron's eyes, steely blue and intently focused, gazing back at her in the rearview mirror, looking at her as he'd asked her questions. A chill shivered through her, and she wasn't so sure that was true about taking control. Not anymore.

Pacific Gardens was nice enough, Alan thought, as those kinds of places went. Spanish in style, with a red tile roof and arches and a tiered fountain in front of the main entrance. The lobby looked more like a middle-to-high-end motel than a rest home, with potted palms and brightly upholstered chairs, and simulated terra-cotta floor tile, no doubt because real Mexican clay pavers would have been unkind to wheelchairs and walkers.

The front desk was manned by a friendly Hispanic woman with a nice smile who greeted Lindsey by name.

As she signed them in, Alan's eye wandered down a wide corridor, where, through open double doors, he could see several of the residents of the facility sitting in wheelchairs, shawl-draped shoulders hunched, gazing blankly at a flickering television screen, frail ghosts of the people they'd once been. He flashed briefly on the two old people in their blood-soaked bed, and knew a moment of not empathy, exactly, but knowledge, at least. Maybe even understanding.

Lindsey beckoned, and he followed her through the lobby, through double glass doors that opened automatically before them, out into spacious grounds, expanses of lawn shaded by huge pines and landscaped with lots of palm trees and bird-of-paradise, bougainvillea and lily-of-the-Nile. Roses and other flowers still bloomed in well-groomed beds, even this late in the fall. Wide pathways of smooth asphalt—again, for the accommodation of wheels and walkers and shuffling feet—wound through the gardens, connecting areas both sunny and shady where benches and tables offered opportunities for rest and reflection.

Yeah, a nice-enough place, he supposed, but it gave him the willies, anyway.

He wondered how much a place like this must cost. Plenty, he was sure. Lindsey had assured him her dad could afford it. He'd been a banker—vice president of something or other—before he'd retired, and had made wise investments, most of which had survived the economic meltdown. He'd also had the foresight to purchase long-term-care insurance, for both himself and his wife, because, Lindsey said, he'd told her he didn't want them to ever be a burden on *her.*

She'd said that with a fierce kind of pride, Alan had noted, as if being a good financial planner was proof positive a man couldn't possibly also be a cold-blooded killer.

"Mom lives in the assisted living section," Lindsey explained as they navigated the curving, branching pathways at a brisk pace. "She has her own apartment—for now. Later, she can be moved into the main building where she would have more supervision and care."

She knocked on the heavy wooden door of a single-story Spanish-style bungalow that appeared to be divided into several small apartments, then called out, "Mom? It's Lindsey." She waited a moment, then took a key out of her pocket and threw an explanation over her shoulder as she unlocked the door. "Being able to lock her door makes her feel safe. I have a key and the staff has one, of course."

"But not your dad," Alan said.

She shook her head, and her voice was low and breathless. "He's not allowed to visit her at all. Can you imagine? She's been married to him for over forty years, and won't even let him come and see her."

She opened the door and stepped into the apartment, calling again, "Mom? Where are you? It's me, Lindsey...."

Behind her in the doorway, Alan paused. Through the tiny living room and an open sliding glass door, he could see a woman in an enclosed patio garden area, surrounded by pots filled with flowering plants. Hearing Lindsey's greeting, she turned, wiping a gloved hand holding a trowel across her forehead. Her face broke into a smile.

"Oh, Lindsey, what a nice surprise. Did you bring me pansies? Oh—" She had started toward her daughter, then caught sight of Alan and hesitated. A look of uncertainty crossed her face—briefly. Then the smile returned, but more polite now—even determined—than pleased. "Oh—I see you've brought a friend." She came in, pulling off her gloves.

"Do I know you?" she asked as she extended a hand to Alan, and her smile grew apologetic. "Forgive me—I forget…things, you know."

"No, ma'am, we haven't met." Alan found that he had softened his voice and was holding her hand gently, the way he would if he were dealing with a victim of violent crime. "I'm Alan. Alan Cameron."

He wasn't sure what he'd expected. Someone older, for sure. He knew, given her daughter's age, that she had to be in her upper sixties, maybe even early seventies—which wasn't all that old nowadays, he reminded himself. It was probably the Alzheimer's association that had him envisioning someone lost-looking, gray-haired and fragile, like the ghosts he'd glimpsed in the recreation room off the front lobby.

Susan Merrill looked far from fragile, though she did have quite a bit of gray in her dark hair, which was thick and shoulder-length, like Lindsey's, but worn in a style reminiscent of another era—a pageboy, he thought it was called. Not exactly up-to-date, but on her it looked right. She was tall, slender and fit-looking, with skin that showed some sun damage—testimony to the fact that she belonged to a generation that had grown up believing a deep tan was a sign of health. Her eyes were fringed with the same dark lashes that made her daughter's so arresting, but their color was hazel, a mix of green and gold that changed with the light.

"Mom," Lindsey said, "this is *Detective* Cameron. He's a policeman."

Susan Merrill gave a faint gasp and jerked her hand back. She looked at her daughter, a brief, startled glance, but Alan thought he saw hope flare in her eyes when they came back to him, just before they changed again and grew shuttered and wary.

"Well, my goodness, isn't that nice," she said, with a new vagueness that Alan thought didn't quite ring true. She turned back toward the patio door, the gloves clutched in her hand fluttering with apparent agitation. "Lindsey, did you bring me pansies? You said you would bring me pansies." Her voice was thin and high, like a child's.

"I brought you pansies yesterday." Lindsey threw Alan a helpless look and went after her mother. "Mom, I told—"

"Well, I used them *all*." Now, the voice was clipped, impatient. "You can see—there, and there and *there*. And I need some more—for these pots, here, you see? I need—"

"I'll bring you some more pansies," Lindsey said wearily. She gently removed the gloves and trowel from her mother's hands and laid them on a wrought-iron patio table, then guided her into a matching chair. "Mom, I told Detective Cameron about your dreams. He wants—"

Susan's sharp bark of laughter interrupted her. "*She* thinks they're dreams," she said angrily to Alan. "They're not *dreams*. They're memories. *Memories*, Detective. I still have some, you know." She looked away, swallowing repeatedly, hands moving restlessly on the wrought-iron tabletop, and after a moment came a whispered, "I *can* remember."

Alan sat in the other chair and leaned toward her, hands clasped loosely between his knees. "What do you remember, Susan?" he asked softly.

She threw him a look full of fear and distrust and shook her head.

Lindsey gave an exasperated hiss and opened her purse.

She took out a small framed photograph, plunked it down on the tabletop in front of her mother, then crouched down beside her chair. "Tell him, Mom. Tell him who this is."

A look of loathing darkened Susan's face. With jerky, uncoordinated movements, she turned the photograph face down on the table and pushed it away from her. "I know who *you* think it is," she said bitterly. And then, to Alan, "*She* thinks I'm crazy. But I'm not. That man—the man in that picture—is the man who killed my husband. And me."

"*Tried* to kill you, Mama," Lindsey said, as she settled into a more comfortable position on the patio pavers.

"Whatever." Susan waved that off as if it were a detail of no importance. "He *shot* me, Detective. I saw his face, as clearly as I see yours." Then she hesitated, looking less sure. "Except…it was dark. I think. Yes—I'm certain it was dark—nighttime. But there was light on his face. I saw *that* face. And then he shot me. And—" She broke off, her face contorted with fear.

"Tell me what you remember," Alan prompted, keeping his voice low so it wouldn't jar her precarious emotional state. He put his hand over hers, quieting their restless movement. "It's all right…you're safe here."

Watching the way those forbidding features seemed to soften when he spoke to her mother, Lindsey felt a peculiar fluttering sensation inside her chest. *How gentle he is. So patient with her.*

But, she reminded herself, he probably had plenty of practice in dealing with emotionally traumatized people. *Just part of his job. A skill he's perfected. His game face.* Her eyes burned, and she tore them away from him and focused instead on a pot filled with blue and yellow pansies.

Her mother glanced down at her with tear-filled eyes, then raised them once more to Alan. "I wish I could remember more. I try, but…just that. He shot me, and then…darkness. *Cold.* I remember being cold, and alone, and *floating.*" She looked up, face alight with triumph. "Yes! I remember floating. Cold, dark, alone…and floating. I think…I must have died. Don't you think so, Detective? Isn't that what death feels like?"

Her eyes searched the detective's austere features as if he must know the answer to that question, to one of humankind's greatest mysteries, and Lindsey fought back a sob. Tears were streaming down her mother's cheeks unchecked, as if she wasn't even aware she was crying. Lindsey's fingers wanted desperately to wipe the tears away. Her arms ached to gather her mother close and rock her like the child she was slowly but surely becoming. She forced herself to stay silent, to sit hunched and still at her mother's feet.

"What do you remember about the time before you were shot?" Alan asked.

"I used to dream…" Her mother's voice was musical, with no trace of the tears, and for a moment it seemed she must not have heard the softly spoken question. "I had dreams…nightmares…that's what Richard said they were. 'Just a bad dream, Susie, go back to sleep.' That's what he'd say, and so I did. And then…" She jerked upright. "One day, I realized it wasn't a dream. I was *remembering.* Only…it was like I was remembering a different life." Her eyes were wide and bewildered. "A life that wasn't mine. I had a different name, a husband—oh, I can see his face so clearly. But I can't remember his *name.* Or mine. *I can't remember my name.*" And now at last a sob came, shaking her slender body like a buffeting wind.

Lindsey drew her legs up, wrapped her arms around them and rested her forehead on her knees. And she heard Alan's gentle voice ask: "Who is Jimmy?"

And there was a gasp, quickly smothered, and laughter mixed with weeping. "Oh, yes, I remember *him*. I had a baby—no, he was older, but a child. A little boy. That was his name—Jimmy. His hair was dark, like mine, but he had such sweet curls. And his eyes were blue, like his father's."

Lindsey jerked her head up at that—she couldn't help it—but her mother's eyes were still riveted on Alan Cameron, as she rocked herself back and forth, as if in the grip of unbearable agony.

"What happened to them, do you know?" She asked it in a voice that was half sob, half whisper. "What happened to my husband…my Jimmy? Did they die, too? It must have been so long ago…but I feel it—" she touched her chest with a doubled fist "—it hurts so *much*. It *hurts*…as if it happened yesterday."

Alan shook his head slowly, but before he could reply, Susan reached out to him, covered his hands with hers, then gripped them tightly. "Can you find them for me? Find out what happened to them? Please…I know I'm losing my mind. In a year…maybe two…I probably won't even care. Before that happens, I just want to know. *I want to know I'm not crazy.*"

Chapter 3

The plans had been made long before. The boat, the darkness, the weights to take the bodies down. Everything went according to plan. Like clockwork.

Excerpt from the confession of Alexi K.
FBI Files, Restricted Access,
Declassified 2010

"So...what do you think? *Is* she crazy?"

Lindsey's voice, speaking aloud the words that had been playing over and over in his own mind, jerked Alan back to the here and now. "What?" he asked, surprised to find they were nearly back to where they'd parked their cars.

She repeated it, her voice hardened by what he knew was only her attempt to mask an excess of emotion.

"She seems lucid," he said, knowing it sounded flat,

uncaring—a shrug in words. But he had his own ways of masking what was going on inside.

"She was having a very good day." Lindsey's lips tightened as she pressed the remote control in her hand. The Mercedes gave a welcoming chirp. She looked at him, squinting as the sun, already low in the west this early in November, struck her full in the face. And caught the look of skepticism he'd been careless enough to let show. "What? Do you think she's faking? Look, I assure you," she said, rushing on before he could reply, "she's been evaluated by doctors—the best. We've gotten second opinions, and thirds. They've done tests." She paused to draw a strengthening breath. "All agree she is in the early to middle stages of Alzheimer's."

The pain in her sun-washed face was hard to look at. But strangely, it was also hard to tear his eyes away. Recognizing that the pull the woman had on him was in danger of becoming a problem, he sucked in a chestful of willpower along with air. "I'm sure she is. Sadly. But maybe just not as far along as she's letting you think she is."

Lindsey paused in the process of digging in her purse for a pair of sunglasses to squint at him again. "So, you think there might be something to her story?"

"I think she remembers something terrible that happened to somebody. The question is who? And when? And where?"

She didn't reply, being preoccupied with rearranging things in the cavernous depths of her purse. She pulled out the photograph of her father and was about to tuck it under her arm to get it out of her way. He held out his hand and said, "Can I see that?"

She glanced at him and handed over the framed photo without comment. He stared at it while she located her sunglasses and put them on, and knew without being able to see them that her eyes had gone wary again and were watching him from behind the dark lenses. There was tension in her body, and she clutched her purse like a shield—or a weapon—the way she had when she'd first come to his office that morning.

Richard Merrill didn't look like anybody's idea of a stone-cold killer—but then, in Alan's experience, the stoniest, coldest killers seldom did. Merrill looked exactly like what he was—a successful banker and family man, now retired to the comforts of suburbia. King of the backyard barbecue. The photo Lindsey had chosen with which to confront her mother was a candid shot rather than a formal portrait, taken at some family outing, probably, a head-and-shoulders shot with blue sky and ocean as a backdrop. Alan's impression was of a man who had been athletic in his youth and, while not yet running to fat, had thickened in the natural way men do as they get older. In the photo, his face was lifted to the sun and his thinning but still adequate salt-and-pepper hair was disarranged by a breeze from the ocean. He looked, Alan thought, like a happy man. A man completely content with his life. His eyes, smile-creased at the corners—

He looked up at Lindsey and tapped the photograph. "Your father's eyes are dark."

"Brown. Yes."

"Yours are—"

"Blue—I know." She made an impatient gesture. "It's possible, you know. For brown-eyed people to have blue-eyed children. If they both carry the recessive gene."

Alan nodded. "True." *But not likely they'd have a child with eyes as vivid a blue as yours.*

"Anyway, what does it matter?" She opened her car

door and tossed her purse onto the passenger seat, then turned back to him, her fair skin flushed with anger. "Do you think I *care* whether or not Richard Merrill is my biological father? Is that what you think this is about? If it was, I could find out easily enough, couldn't I, through DNA. *That man*—" she nodded at the photograph in his hands, and her voice quivered "—is my dad in every way that counts. I'm not doing this for *me*, I'm doing it for *him*—because he doesn't deserve to be shut out of what life my mother has left. And I'm doing it for *her*, because she doesn't deserve to spend the time she has left being terrified of the husband who adores her. Do you understand?"

"Yes, I do," Alan said, and meant it. He understood very well what she wanted; he just wasn't sure he could give it to her.

"So? Are you going to help me?"

He let out a gusty breath, looked down at the photo in his hands. *Lord, help me,* he thought. He shook his head, but said, "I'll see what I can find out. Can I keep this?"

"Oh—of course. Yes. Sure." She held herself still, but he could almost feel her vibrating with suppressed hope. "Anything I can do to help…"

"We've got the approximate *when*—roughly forty years ago, right? It would help a lot if we could narrow it down as to the *where*. What we're doing is looking for a needle in a haystack, in a whole damn field of haystacks. It would be nice if we knew which haystack to start looking in."

She gave a shrug and a helpless little laugh, and something about the sound of it made him wonder if, behind those sunglasses, she might be crying. "How do I do that?" Her voice was barely a whisper. "You saw her… heard her."

"Yeah, I did. And just talking to us, she remembered a

detail that seemed to be new to her, didn't she? That thing about floating. You said you visit her just about every day, right? See if you can get her to talk about her life before the trauma. Maybe she'll remember some little thing that will help us pinpoint where this thing happened. Can you do that?"

She nodded, quick and hard. "Yes—okay."

"Good. Meanwhile, I'll start running what we have through our various databases. See if anything pops up. Okay?" He waited—one hand on the top of the car door— while she slid behind the wheel and put the key in the ignition. The engine fired, and she settled back in her seat and looked up at him.

"Thank you," she said. Just that.

He couldn't even see her eyes. But something about her mouth…the hint of a flush beneath her skin, a touch of pink on the tip of her nose. He felt a thickening in his throat, a tightening in his chest, and for a long moment couldn't make himself look away. Couldn't seem to move. The moment stretched, then snapped with a sizzling he could feel in his scalp, like the warning tingle just before an electric shock, the one that makes you jerk your hand away just in time.

"Okay, then," he said. "I'll call if I find anything." He took a card and a pencil out of his jacket pocket, jotted his cell phone number on the back of the card and handed it to her. "You do the same."

She nodded. He shut the car door, then stepped back and watched her back out of the parking spot and drive away. He looked down at the photograph of Richard Merrill in his hand, and felt excitement stir and his pulses quicken. And wondered whether it had more to do with the possibility of a very cold case, or a very warm and desirable woman.

* * *

Back at his desk, Alan scanned the photo of Richard Merrill and entered it and all the information Lindsey had given him on her parents into the system, started a data search, then turned his attention to writing the reports on the Marchetti case.

His plan was to finish the report and get a head start on the weekend, since it was his weekend to have Chelse. He'd been thinking about maybe taking her to Sea World or the zoo while the weather was holding so fine. Chelse loved the zoo, always had—Sea World, too—but the way she was growing up, Alan figured it was only a matter of time before she started thinking she was too old for that stuff. He hoped it wouldn't happen, but was realistic enough to know it always did.

Maybe, he thought, he'd get lucky and Chelse would stay her daddy's little girl forever. Maybe, like Lindsey Merrill, she'd still think he walked on water when she was forty. Although he considered the odds of that weren't good, being as how he only got to spend every other weekend with her. It was hard to admit, even to himself, how much he looked forward to those weekends. How much he looked forward to not going home to his empty house.

Even more so this weekend, he realized. For some reason.

He found himself wondering whether Lindsey liked the zoo. Or Sea World. His mind flashed on an image of the three of them—him, Chelse and Lindsey—strolling the wide, eucalyptus-shaded avenues of Balboa Park. Just a flash, and then his mind said, *Nope. Bad idea. Are you nuts?*

All the same, he was glad it was Chelse's weekend. And, he reminded himself, if anything interesting popped up in her parents' backgrounds, he would have a real reason to call Lindsey.

Maybe Sunday.

As it turned out, none of the things he'd planned on doing with his weekend came to pass. He didn't take Chelsea to the zoo or Sea World, didn't see her at all, in fact. Nor did he go home to his empty house, call Lindsey Merrill, or even check back to see what his search had turned up. Because the shooting of Juan Miguel Alviera was only the opening salvo in what came to be called, in the news media, at least, the East Village War.

At six-thirty Friday evening, two carloads of Alviera's homies from the Eastside Diablos armed with automatic weapons shot up a fast-food restaurant where the suspected perpetrators of the Alviera homicide, members of the rival East Village gang known as the Calle Reyes Amigos, were enjoying dinner. One of the Amigos was killed, the other escaped unharmed. Seven innocent bystanders were wounded, three seriously. And the city's barrios—which had been enjoying steadily declining gang violence rates since the horrendous highs of the early 90s, thanks to the combined efforts of the SDPD's gang suppression unit, the DEA and the FBI—erupted.

All patrol personnel, plus the gang and homicide units, were called out in force in an effort to nip the flare-up before it could escalate into all-out war. Alan called Chelsea's mother to tell her he wouldn't be able to take her for the weekend, and prepared to bed down on the couch of a friend who lived in the central city. Chelsea's mom wasn't happy about having to cancel the plans she and her current husband had made to go away for the weekend, and made sure he heard all over again each and every one of the reasons why she'd divorced him in the first place, and why nobody in their right mind should ever marry a cop. But what could he do?

On Saturday, the Amigos retaliated against the Whataburger shooters by crashing a wedding of one of the shooter's sisters, at which the shooter was the best man. The hail of automatic weapons fire did manage to take out the best man, and also sent the groom, three wedding guests, and the six-year-old flower girl—the bride's niece—to the hospital with major injuries.

Whether it was the shock of that tragedy—augmented by photos splashed all over the media, of the little girl in her blood-soaked flower girl's dress—or the SDPD sweep that hauled in off the streets every known affiliate of the two rival gangs that could be found, by Sunday night things had settled down. The thinking behind the sweep was, by the time the collars had all been sorted out and processed—most back to the streets of their respective neighborhoods—passions would probably have cooled off some. At least for the time being.

Sunday night, home for a shower and change of clothes, Alan called the hospital to check on the flower girl. He was told she was "critical but stable—holding her own."

Lindsey couldn't decide what to do. At least a dozen times she'd picked up the card with the penciled phone number on the back and stared at it. And a dozen times had put it back on her desk without dialing. She'd done it so many times, the number was now etched in her memory. Why couldn't she bring herself to call him?

It was true that Alan—Detective Cameron—had told her to call him if she found out anything that might help narrow down the location of the traumatic events in her mother's past. But this was such a *small* thing. Would he think it significant enough to warrant bothering him on a weekend? He had made it pretty clear he was looking into this without much enthusiasm or real hope of success. And he had said he would call her if *he* found anything. Which meant, since she hadn't heard from him, that he didn't have anything to tell her. She didn't want to be a pest.

Oh, grow up, Lindsey. At least be honest with yourself. You know the real reason you can't let yourself call the man is because you want to so badly.

There. She'd done it—spoken inside her head the truth she'd been trying not to acknowledge. She wanted to call Detective Alan Cameron. Wanted to hear his voice again. Better yet, wanted to see him again.

His face hovered in her mind wherever she went, whatever she did, always there, following her the way she used to think the moon followed her when she was a little girl. His eyes…the unexpected softness that came into them when he spoke to her mother, in such stark contrast with the hardness, the speculation, the cop look that was there all the rest of the time. She wondered what it would be like to see that softness when he looked at *her*.

Silly, of course. So very junior high school. She'd just barely met the man. Ridiculously, demoralizingly stupid to have his voice, the words and phrases he'd spoken, playing over and over in her mind like a song that had gotten stuck there.

She wasn't sure what she was going to do about it, but one thing she was *not* going to do was make an idiot of herself over a man she didn't even know. And a *cop*, for God's sake!

It had been such a long time since any man had made an impression on her—why did it have to be a cop?

Needing to get out of the house, away from the phone and the temptation it presented, she changed her clothes and went out for a run along the cliffs, taking her house key on a chain around her neck as she always did and leaving everything else, even her cell phone, behind.

Tomorrow, she told herself as she ran. *Monday, a work day—will be better. I'll have plenty of things to distract me—with any luck, a flood or a hurricane or some sort of disaster. You know I don't mean that, God, right? And if he hasn't called by the end of the work day, well, that's a reasonable length of time to wait.*

She felt better, somehow, having made that decision. Stronger. More disciplined. *If he hasn't called by five o'clock Monday, I will call him.*

Monday morning when Alan reported in, police headquarters was still a zoo. But at least there hadn't been any more shootings overnight. No more bodies. *Thank you, Lord.*

By around four o'clock, with the short November afternoon already sliding toward dusk and the lights in the squad room turning the windows to mirrors, he finally found a moment to see what the make he'd run on Richard and Susan Merrill had turned up. He wasn't expecting much—was pretty sure he knew what he was going to find—nothing. No warrants, no arrests, no priors. The Merrills were undoubtedly exactly what they seemed to be: Two nice, law-abiding, upper-middle-class Americans with no more than the usual number of skeletons in their family closets. Sad about the wife's Alzheimer's, but, those things happened, even to nice people.

For a few minutes after he brought up the screen, his sleep-deprived mind refused to process what he was seeing.

He read through the results for Susan Merrill, then for Richard, scrolled back to the beginning of Susan's and read through both again. Nope—he hadn't missed anything. He tipped back his chair and gazed at the data neatly boxed and itemized on the screen, frowning and tapping a pencil on his desktop. He straightened abruptly and reached for his phone, but hung it up without dialing and shoved back his chair instead. A few minutes later he was knocking on the door of his captain's office.

Getting the answer he usually did—an unintelligible growl—Alan opened the door, stuck his head through the crack and said, "Sir, got a minute?"

Captain Ron Tupman hitched back in his chair and snapped, "Just about that much."

Alan gave him about half a grin. "Yeah, been a crazy couple of days, hasn't it?" Captain Tupman was in charge of both the gang and homicide units, among others. "If you'd rather not—"

"Already got my attention, don't wimp out now." The captain tossed a pen onto the mess of paperwork on his desk. "What's on your mind, Detective Cameron?"

Alan filled him in, beginning with Lindsey Merrill's visit and ending with the results of the background search on Richard and Susan Merrill. The captain listened without interrupting, a habit that was one of the things Alan liked and respected about the man, and no doubt at least part of the reason why he was currently occupying an office with a nameplate on the door.

"Now that things have settled down a bit, if you can spare me, I'd like to take a couple of days to follow up on it," Alan concluded. "See where it goes."

Captain Tupman stuck out his lower lip and contemplated the mess on his desk for a full ten seconds. Then he leaned forward and picked up the pen. "This mess is Gang Unit's headache, they're coordinating with the feds, so yeah, unless any more bodies turn up, might as well go with it." He looked up and leveled his patented black stare at Alan. "If this thing grows legs, I want to know about it."

"Sure—you bet. Thanks." Alan was on his way out the door when his cell phone vibrated against his side. He waved an apology and a farewell to his captain and exited, glancing at the caller ID as he thumbed the talk button. He didn't recognize the number immediately, but somehow knew it was Lindsey, and was surprised by the little zap of electricity that shot through him. Not adrenaline—he got enough of that in his job and it wasn't a sensation he enjoyed, not like some thrill junkies he knew. This was different—and entirely pleasant.

"Hey," he said, after she'd identified herself in a hushed and breathless voice, as if she were doing something illicit, "I was just going to call you."

Lindsey felt quivery inside. "Oh," she said, and laughed. She took the phone away from her ear to check. But the hand holding it appeared to be steady. She cleared her throat, and when she spoke, so did he.

They both said together, "Did you find something?" And Lindsey laughed and said, "You first."

"Uh-uh," Alan said, "you called me. You go first."

Her heart was pounding. She thought, *This is silly. I'm being silly.* "I don't know if it's any help. It probably isn't."

"Why don't you tell me and let me decide?"

She took a breath, closed her eyes and said, "Snow."

"Snow?"

"I told you. It's probably nothing. My mother says she remembers Jimmy liked to play in the snow. At first, I thought, at least that tells us it wasn't in San Diego. But then I realized, you can drive a couple of hours from here and be in snow. *I've* played in the snow. So maybe…"

"Yeah," he said. He sounded distracted, and again Lindsey thought, *Stupid, stupid. I'm wasting his time.* Then he said, "Look, I need to talk to you. How about if I meet you somewhere?"

A breath gusted through her like a freshening wind off the ocean, chilling her, but at the same time filling her with what could only be described as *joy.* She tried to believe the cause was the thought that he must have found some information on her mother's memories, but she knew it wasn't only that. She wasn't in the habit of kidding herself. This *thing* she was feeling, this junior high school excitement, or whatever it was, was because she was going to see Alan again.

Demoralizing, she thought, for a forty-year-old businesswoman who should certainly know better. She was being ridiculous and in grave danger of making a fool of herself. She had to get a grip, *now.*

The silence on the phone had lasted no more than a moment. "Tell you what," she said, and was pleased and a little surprised at how calm and adult her voice sounded. "I'm about to go for a run. Why don't you meet me at Sunset Cliffs Park? By the time you get there I should be about finished." *There,* she thought. That should demonstrate that she wasn't falling all over herself to accommodate him.

And, she thought, a brisk run along the cliffs should give her a chance to expend some nervous energy and get her head on straight. A good dose of endorphins was just what she needed.

Her heart lurched into her throat as she realized he'd

said something that hadn't registered. "What?" she asked, feeling rattled again.

"Where, exactly? That's a mile and a half of cliffs."

"Uh, okay, how about the little parking lot just north of the rock where the peace sign used to be. Do you know the one—"

"I know it well," Alan said. "I'm on my way."

The sun was setting when Alan pulled into the postage stamp of a parking lot wedged between Sunset Cliffs Boulevard and the cliff's edge. After parking and turning off the motor, for a few moments he just sat in his car, taking in the spectacle of the sun setting into the Pacific Ocean, missing the dark silhouette of the peace sign that had once—briefly—graced the top of the forty-foot rock formation, before mysteriously disappearing one January night. *Too bad,* he thought. Somehow, maybe, that universal symbol of peace and brotherhood would have helped to cancel out some of the ugliness of his weekend.

He got out of his car, then realized the ocean breeze had grown chilly with the going of the sun and took his jacket out of the backseat and put it on. Leaning against the car with his back to the fading sunset, he watched joggers chugging past on the dirt pathway that wound along the cliffs. Anticipation raced under his skin, ebbing and flowing like the waves beating against the rocks far below as each runner hove into view, then drew close enough for him to see it wasn't the one he was waiting for. When he did finally see the lone figure bobbing toward him, coming from the south, he knew her instantly, even in silhouette against the lavender sky.

She was wearing sweats and a tank top, and had a warmup jacket tied around her waist by its arms. She was also wearing a sun visor, which she took off as she veered into the parking lot, leaving a sweatband in place, stark white against her dark hair.

She slowed to a walk and her face broke into a smile. "Hi—been waiting long?"

The smile had accomplished, it seemed, what the sunset and the missing peace sign hadn't been able to, because he found himself wearing a smile, too, and there was a lightness in his heart for no particular reason he could think of.

He shook his head, then nodded toward the two other cars in the lot. "Which one's yours?"

"Neither." She wiped sweat from her face with a dangling sleeve of the warm-up jacket, seemingly only a little winded from her run. "I live about half a mile north of here. I usually run down to the stairs at the southern end of the park and back, which is about three miles. If I want a longer run, I go to Pacific Beach or Mission Bay."

"Lucky you," Alan said. He nodded toward the darkening cliffs, and the sea still gilded with the remains of the sunset. "This is one of my favorite places. I bring Chelse here sometimes. You know—to explore the caves and tidepools."

She untied the warm-up jacket, then gave him a startled look when he took it from her and held it for her so she could slip her arms into the sleeves. So close to her he could feel the moist heat rising from her body, he felt her shiver suddenly.

"Why don't we sit in the car out of the wind," he said. "You don't want to get chilled."

She nodded, and he opened the passenger-side door, waited for her to settle into the seat, then closed the door and went around and got behind the wheel. He closed the door and the dusk and the quiet and an unexpected sense of intimacy enveloped them. And for a moment, for some reason, he couldn't think what he'd come to say.

Lindsey stared through the windshield at the darkening sky, listening to the thumping of her own heart. Other than that, the silence seemed profound, and she thought, *This is weird. One of us has to say something.* And felt herself on the edge of panic, unable to think of anything.

But then, miraculously, she heard herself say, in that blessedly calm and grown-up voice that came from she knew not where, "What was it you wanted to tell me? The reason you wanted to meet me."

Instead of answering her question, he looked at her and said abruptly, "Tell me more about the snow."

"There isn't any more. Just that." She shrugged. "Mom said Jimmy loved to play in the snow. That she would dress him in his snowsuit and he looked like a fat little penguin." She looked at him expectantly, and her heart continued to beat too fast.

He let out a hissing breath and for a few long moments, just stared out at the ocean and sky. Finally, he glanced over at her, and in the remaining light she could see the frown on his face. "Before she got sick, did your mother ever talk about her childhood? When she was a girl? Did she have any photographs? Mementos? High school yearbooks?"

Her stomach gave a queer little lurch. She looked at him for a moment, then shook her head and looked away. "I used to ask about that. Mom would just laugh and make some general remarks about being a bookworm, not very popular—which I always thought hard to believe, since she was—" she caught a quick, painful breath "—so beautiful. If I pressed her for more details, she would get upset and sort of look to my dad for help. So…" She paused again, this time to clear her throat, to give a small laugh of apology. "I'm sorry," she said, "I didn't think this was going to be so hard."

He nodded and murmured something encouraging, and after a moment she went on.

"Anyway, one day he took me aside and explained that there had been a house fire when my mother was still in her teens and that everything was lost, including both her parents. Mom was injured—she has a scar on one side of her head. The way she wears her hair, you can't see it at all. Dad says there's a lot she doesn't remember about her childhood. So, naturally, it was upsetting for her to talk about. After that..." She shrugged.

After that, she'd never asked again. But she remembered still the feeling of walls going up and doors slamming shut. She almost told Alan about that, and about the nightmares she'd had for a long time after, of watching her mother slide away from her down a long, long corridor, growing smaller and smaller, until she could barely see her, and crying out to her to come back, and feeling bereft, like a small child abandoned in the woods. She'd never told anyone, not even her husband, about that dream, or the loneliness she'd felt then. What would make her think *this* man, a police detective with a hard face and sharp eyes, might understand?

"Why?" Her voice was harsh because of the ache in her throat.

Instead of answering, he muttered, "That could explain it." He sounded distracted, distant, and the impulse to bare her soul to him vanished like smoke. "Maybe."

He was silent for a moment, then abruptly shifted in his seat, turning so he almost faced her, left arm draped across the steering wheel. "You wanted to know what I've found out so far. The truth is, precious little. In fact, Lindsey, according to public records, your mother, Susan Merrill, didn't exist before roughly forty years ago when she appeared in San Diego as the wife of Richard Merrill."

Chapter 4

The man...was very protective of her. He tried always to put his body between his wife and my gun. As if flesh could stop bullets.
Excerpt from the confession of Alexi K.
FBI Files, Restricted Access,
Declassified 2010

"I don't understand," Lindsey said. She felt sick. "What do you mean, she didn't exist? How is that possible?"

"Not literally, of course, just according to public record."

"But, I told you, there was a fire—"

"And that could explain it," Alan said, cutting her off. But it was plain to her that it didn't explain it, not to his satisfaction.

Anger filled her, although she didn't know quite where to direct it; she'd asked for this herself, after all. "What about my dad?" she asked, keeping her voice under tight control. "I know there's stuff about him. I've seen it."

"Oh, sure there is. Birth certificate says he was born in a little town somewhere in Nebraska."

She nodded, fidgety now with a nervous excitement she couldn't account for. "Yes—that's where he grew up. He played high school sports—mostly football, I think. He was even student body president, prom king—the whole thing. I've seen his yearbook," she added with an emphasis that bordered on belligerent.

"Yeah, the only problem with that is," Alan said, reaching to turn on the ignition, "the Nebraska town where Richard Merrill supposedly did all those things was wiped off the map by a tornado in the nineteen-fifties."

He didn't look at her, and in the dashboard light his profile appeared grim, even menacing. She told herself it was only the way the shadows played across his rather sharp features, but she was shaking again, hugging herself inside the warm-up jacket to try to make herself stop it. "So?"

He swept her with a glance as he backed out of the parking space. "So, there's no way to verify any of it, except maybe to try to track down some of the town's former residents and see if any of them remember Richard Merrill and his family. I'm thinking there's a pretty slim chance of that, after more than half a century."

"I don't believe this," Lindsey muttered, staring out at the palm trees and pricey ocean-view houses slipping past the car window. It was beginning to seem to her like a bad dream. Her mother's delusions, the Alzheimer's—that had been hard to take. But this didn't even seem real. "Look—I know my dad didn't do this thing—whatever it is my mother thinks he did. He's just not—he *couldn't* have. You'd have to know him. If you did, then maybe you'd understand—*he did...not...do...this.*"

He nodded. "I am going to need to talk to him." He heard the sharp intake of breath and glanced over at her. "You know that, don't you?"

"Yes. Just...please not yet. Okay? Not...yet."

He swore silently to himself. Wished he wasn't driving. Wished for better light. Wanted—needed to see her face, to see if the fear he was hearing in her voice was reflected there, too. Was it just the fear of a daddy's girl afraid of hurting or disappointing the parent she adored, or something else? Being a cop, he knew he was programmed by experience to expect the darkest. The ugliest. The worst.

"Why not?" he asked gently.

She exhaled again, slowly this time. "It's just that...I haven't told him about...um, that I've talked to the police about this. And I don't want to, not until I have something I can tell him, some kind of explanation for my mother's dreams, some reason for the way she's been behaving. I don't want him to think I—" She stopped there and half turned in her seat to look at him. "Do you understand?"

Alan put one hand over his mouth and shook his head. But he knew better than to press her; she already felt bad enough, he could tell. She was a people-pleaser by nature. Even without looking directly at her he could feel her eyes on his face, begging him to understand. He did, of course—probably better than she knew.

"Oh—this is my street. Left here..." And her voice sounded diffident, as if she knew she'd disappointed him and was unsure where she stood with him now.

The turn took him into the entry driveway of a gated town-house complex—although the low picket fence

Memory of Murder

appeared to be more for decoration than security. Lindsey pulled a key attached to a chain around her neck out of the front of her tank top. Also on the chain was a small remote control. She aimed it at the gate, which promptly swung inward to admit them. He drove through into a park-like area landscaped with eucalyptus and other evergreen shrubs and trees he couldn't identify in the dark. The buildings, lit by sidewalk lamps and sconces mounted on the walls, were two-story and modern in style, with stuccoed chimneys and fake-wood shingle roofs made of something no doubt impervious to fire.

He gave a low whistle of appreciation. "Ocean view. Must be nice."

She seemed to take that as a criticism of some kind, and replied with an edge of defensiveness, "I bought it after my divorce. I had no husband, no children, nobody to please but myself. Since I love the ocean, why not live close to it?" She threw him a look and a wry smile. "My dad helped me finance it, naturally. And of course this was before the big real estate boom. Right now, after the crash, I figure it's probably worth fairly close to what I originally paid for it. That's mine right there. You can pull into the driveway, if you—" She gave a sharp gasp, having just noticed, as Alan had, that the driveway in question was already occupied by a light-colored luxury sedan.

She uttered a sibilant swear word that both surprised and delighted him. Up to that point, she'd seemed almost too "good," in the moralistic sense, to be true, little Miss Goody Two-shoes determined to be on her best behavior, minding all her p's and q's. That one word banished the illusion and made her more *real* to him, meaning the opposite of fake, not fantasy. Or, he thought, maybe human was the better word. Less reserved. More…touchable.

"It's my *dad*," she whispered, throwing him a look that was close to panic. "Quick—drive on! Drive on!"

"I think it's too late," Alan said. He was watching a man coming down the driveway, dressed in khakis, hands in the pockets of his unzipped windbreaker. He'd halted when he saw Alan's car slow at the foot of the driveway; now he pulled a hand from a pocket to shade his eyes from the headlights, then broke into a smile. "I think he's made you."

As far as Alan was concerned, the chance meeting couldn't have been better. Save him some time and trouble, it seemed to him. Obviously, Lindsey wasn't of the same mind. The face she turned to him wore an expression of dread.

"What am I going to do? How am I going to explain this? How do I explain *you?*"

Part of him was getting tired of having to tiptoe around Daddy-dear in this investigation; as far as Alan was concerned, the guy was a possible suspect in a very old possible homicide, and the sooner he was able to get a fix on the man, the better. But there was another part of him—small, but developing an alarmingly loud voice—that seemed to want to protect this woman from pain and anguish if he possibly could.

The man in the driveway—Richard Merrill—had given them a friendly wave and was now standing with hands once more shoved into the pockets of his windbreaker, obviously waiting for them—or his daughter, at least—to get out of the car. Alan pulled past the driveway and parked, then produced a big smile and a friendly wave back.

"Follow my lead," he said to Lindsey from behind the smile, without moving his lips. He put his hand on her shoulder and felt her flinch nervously at his touch. "Don't freak out. I'm just going to kiss you."

Her face jerked toward him. He saw her eyes widen, glistening in the light from the sidewalk lamps. He heard her sip in a breath as he leaned across the center console, and then her lips were warm and soft against his. He was prepared for that. What he wasn't prepared for was the thump inside his chest, and the power surge that went zinging through all the nerves and muscles in his body.

It took all the willpower he had not to slide his hand along her shoulder and up under her hair, then hold her head still and press into the kiss until she got over the shock of it and began to kiss him back. Instead, he pulled away just far enough to whisper, "You okay with this?"

She nodded—just barely. He could feel her body trembling under his hand. He could feel his own heart pounding as he murmured, "You get where I'm going?"

This time she managed a firmer nod, along with a shaky laugh.

"Okay, then." He gave her shoulder a squeeze, then turned and opened the car door. He got out, calling a friendly, "Hello there!" to Richard Merrill.

He made his way around to the passenger side, where Lindsey was in the process of exiting the vehicle. As soon as she'd cleared the door and shut it behind her, he reached out and put his arm around her. "Busted," he said to her with wry good humor, as he pulled her in close to his side. "Looks like I'm finally going to get to meet your dad."

Lindsey angled a look at him, then gave an uneasy-sounding laugh. "Uh, Dad...this is Alan Cameron. Alan, meet Richard Merrill—my dad."

Alan stepped forward, bringing Lindsey with him. Since she was snuggled in next to his body, he could feel she was still trembling—or vibrating with tension—as he leaned and held out his hand. Smiling with teeth showing, he said, "It's good to finally meet you, sir. Lindsey's told me so much about you."

Richard Merrill shook his hand but his smile was more cautious than friendly, and his voice was not warm. "I wish I could say the same. Lindsey?"

"Dad, I'm sorry, I was going to tell you, I just…" She looked at Alan again, clearly unsure where she was supposed to go now. He gazed back at her, smiling reassuringly. "Uh…the thing is, you see…"

"The thing is, Mr. Merrill," he said, taking the reins from her again, "I'm a police detective."

"Really." Merrill did a little startled pullback, which didn't mean all that much to Alan; he got that sort of reaction a lot.

"Quite frankly," Alan went on, "Linz didn't know how you'd feel about your daughter dating a cop."

Merrill rubbed at the back of his neck. "Quite frankly, I'm not sure how I feel about that, myself. How long have you two been…uh, dating?"

Alan and Lindsey both started to speak, then stopped and looked at each other. Alan said, "I don't know…what has it been? About a month?"

"More like two," she said, getting into the game enough to give him a playful nudge. Although laying it on a little heavy, he thought.

He grinned at her. "Seems a lot shorter." The glint in her eyes…was it a trick of the light, or could it possibly be laughter? He found himself holding his breath to contain the urge to laugh with her, laugh with sheer delight and the same sense of discovery he'd felt when he'd heard her swear out loud.

"How did you meet my daughter, Detective?"

Merrill's voice startled him; for a moment the world had seemed to include only two people.

Lindsey laughed. "Dad, what is this? What am I, sixteen?"

"No, honey, it's okay. Mr. Merrill, I'd want to know, if it was my daughter. Here's the story. I went to her office looking to get a better deal on my car insurance. Someone I know on the job had recommended her to me. Wound up insuring my car and my house, and we've been seeing each other ever since." He hugged Lindsey even closer to his side, and couldn't help but notice she didn't seem to mind. And that the trembling had diminished. Maybe she was getting over the strangeness of him, beginning to relax a little bit? The idea of that pleased him a lot more than it should have.

Merrill appeared to relax a little, as well. "Well, as long as Lindsey's happy, I'm glad to meet you, Alan—and I'm Richard, by the way." He paused. "Detective, you said? What kind?"

"Homicide."

"Really?" He did that little rearing back, startle thing again. "Well, at least it's not drugs or vice. Or gangs. Speaking of which—terrible thing that happened this past weekend, wasn't it?"

"Yes, sir," Alan said, "it was."

Merrill appeared to be about to ask another question, but Lindsey interrupted. "What are you doing here, Dad? Not that I'm not glad to see you."

He pointed an accusing finger at his daughter. "Now, I tried to call you. I did. You weren't answering your cell phone."

"Dad, you know I don't take it when I go running."

Merrill looked at Alan and raised both hands in a gesture of paternal helplessness. "What am I gonna do with her? You're a cop, tell her how nuts she is to go out alone like that without a cell phone!"

"Dad, it's not like I'm out in the wilderness. Where I run it's on a busy street with houses on the other side, people all over the place, jogging, walking their dogs, playing with their kids. It's perfectly safe. And," she added in a wry aside to Alan, loud enough for her father to hear, "I'm forty years old, for Pete's sake."

"And you're never going to be too old for your dad to worry about you—don't you forget that." Merrill gave Alan a narrow look. "You have children, son?"

"Yes sir, I do," Alan said. "A daughter—she's almost ten."

"Ah. Then you know—or if you don't now, you will." He took a set of keys out of his pocket and peeped open his car door locks, then turned back to them. "I was in the neighborhood and thought I'd stop by since I couldn't get you on the phone. Wanted to see if you feel like coming over on the weekend."

He smiled, but now Alan thought it seemed forced... awkward. And it struck him suddenly, with a flash of unwanted sympathy, what it must be like for a man married for more than forty years, suddenly finding himself without his wife. It was pretty obvious to him the man was lonely.

"You know, thought I might warm up the old barbecue, invite some of the neighbors, be like old times. Before your mother..." He cleared his throat, then threw Alan a fierce look. "I suppose she's told you—"

"Yes," Alan said. "I'm sorry. Must be tough." What else could he say?

Lindsey had opened her mouth to reply, but before she could, Richard Merrill said to Alan, "You're included in the invitation, of course."

Her head snapped toward Alan and her eyes widened, the look she gave him saying plainly, *Oh, no! What now?*

He was asking himself that same question. The invitation was a golden opportunity, the perfect chance for him to learn more about the elusive Merrills, but the timing couldn't have been worse. He said in a murmur meant only for Lindsey, "I have Chelsea that weekend."

Naturally, Merrill overheard. "Chelsea? That would be your daughter?"

"Yes, sir. I was supposed to have her last weekend, but after all hell broke loose in the 'hood, I had to cancel. I can't disappoint her again."

"No, no—by all means, bring her along. I have a pool, some of the neighbors have kids, grandkids. She'll be more than welcome. She'll have fun. So, what do you say? Can I count on the three of you?"

Lindsey popped open her mouth and threw Alan that *Help-me-out-and-don't-you-dare-say-yes!* look again.

"Sure," he said. "We'd love to come. We'll be there."

He heard a little gasp, then a bright and artificially cheery, "O-*kay!* So, Dad, I guess that's, um… So, we'll see you next what, Saturday? What time?" He could hear a note of desperation in her voice, and feel those ripples of tension cascading through her body again.

Interesting.

Merrill shrugged and divided a look between the two of them. "Around two? It gets dark so early this time of year."

"Two's fine with me," Alan said.

"Two it is," Lindsey almost sang, and Alan snugged her a little closer still.

Then he had to let go of her momentarily as her father stepped forward to give her a hug and a kiss on the forehead. "That's great—just great. See you Saturday, then. Good to meet you, Alan." He clapped Alan on his upper arm, got into his car and backed out of the driveway.

Alan and Lindsey waved, then stood together and silently watched the big sedan roll through the automatic gate that had opened to let it pass, pause, taillights winking, then turn right and move off down the street. It was only then, with the quiet of the empty driveway and spotlighted landscaping shadows settling in around them, that he realized his arm was encircling her again. That somehow, for some reason, she'd moved right back into the curve of his body, into the place she'd vacated to accept her father's farewell hug. He wondered if she'd done it without thinking, because it felt natural and right, the way it had felt so natural and right to him he hadn't given it a thought, either.

They broke apart at what seemed like the same moment—impossible to tell who did it first.

Lindsey gave a little laugh, sounding half relieved, half embarrassed. "Boy, you do that well."

"What?"

"Lie."

That stopped him for a moment, making him do his own little mental rearing back, the word an unexpected jolt to his self-image. He lied on a daily basis, of course, dealing with suspects and witnesses alike, and never gave it a thought. Went with the territory. He did and said what was necessary to get the job done, and it wasn't always one hundred percent gospel truth. He sure didn't think it made him any less of a good guy.

His chuckle was self-deprecating. "Think he bought it?"

She hugged herself, rubbing her upper arms inside the sleeves of the warm-up jacket, although the evening wasn't that chilly. "Why wouldn't he? I'm forty years old—I'm sure the notion that I might bring a man home with me occasionally isn't *that* shocking." Her voice sounded clipped, almost angry.

"Do you?"

"Do I what?"

"Bring men home with you...occasionally?"

She gave a little start, in a way that reminded him of her father. "What earthly business is that of yours?"

He held up his hands in mock surrender. "Hey, if we're supposed to be, uh, *dating*, I just figured I ought to know what I'm getting into."

The fact that she was being teased sank in, and she made a small sound, a snort, and gave him a sideways glaring look to go with it. After a moment, she pulled off the sweatband and raked her fingers through her hair, then suddenly held her head between her hands and let go of an exasperated breath. "But, *why* did you say we'd go to the barbecue? You realize, we're going to have to keep up the charade of us being a couple all afternoon. And what about your daughter? What's she going to think?"

"About what?"

"Well, me, obviously. The fact that we're supposedly uh, dating...."

"She's ten, Lindsey. Who I happen to be *dating* is no concern of hers."

"Oh," she said, arching her eyebrows at him, "so *are*

you dating someone?" Before he could answer, she gave an elaborate shrug and added, "I just figured, you know, since *we're* supposed to be dating, I ought to know what I'm getting into."

He grinned to show his appreciation of the small *gotcha*, and she grinned back. And it occurred to him, as it did each time he was with her, that he was enjoying himself entirely too much, given the nature of their relationship.

He coughed and folded his arms and planted his feet, adopting a classic cop stance to remind himself again what that relationship was. "Look, it's the perfect opportunity dumped right in my lap. You bet I'm going to take it. I need to talk to your father, you don't want me to talk to him—not like a cop, and I understand that. So, this is my chance to talk to him without arousing his suspicions. Casual conversation—*you* know. I'm in a relationship with his daughter, what could be more natural than to want to know more about her family? I'm sure he's going to want to know all about me, so, I tell him about growing up in Philly, and I ask him where he grew up. It's tit for tat." He smiled at her, not with amusement. "Plus, it's a great opportunity for you to show me those high school yearbooks you were telling me about."

She gazed at him, not saying anything, eyes fringed in darkness, reflecting the light. Then she nodded and murmured, "Okay, you're right. Of course." He could hear the faint *plink* of her swallow.

"Meanwhile, I'll keep looking, see if I come up with anything. Are you going to be seeing your mother this week?"

"Of course. I go almost every day after work."

"Okay, then you keep trying to get her to remember things about her dreams. Let me know immediately if you get anything. Anything—no matter how small or insignificant it might seem to you. Call me."

She nodded, then gave a small laugh. "So, I guess the snow thing wasn't much help, was it?"

"Don't say that." His voice had gone low and husky, entirely without his permission. "You never know."

And then, because just saying good-night to her and walking away didn't seem like enough, he reached out and brushed the bridge of her nose with his thumb.

He heard a soft intake of breath, and that moment in the car, when he'd leaned over and kissed her as part of a charade, came thundering back into his consciousness. A stampede of images, emotions, sensations, things he hadn't had time then to process, hurtled through his mind and for a few seconds, trampled out reason. He was left with a churned-up mess of sensory impressions—soft lips and warm, damp skin and the scent of a clean woman's sweat, and the hint—just the hint—of what it would be like to have those mingling, merging, melding with his own amid the thumping, pulsing rhythms of joined bodies and dueling heartbeats.

He shook his head, shaking off the images and a hint of dizziness. "So," he said in a voice still raspy with the residue of the stampede, "I'll call you. And see you on Saturday." He left her standing there, walked to his car, got in and managed to get his car turned around and heading back through the automatic gate without clipping a shrub or running over the curb.

Entirely too much, he told himself as he bumped a right turn into the street. *Considering the nature of our relationship.*

* * *

Lindsey stood on a wooden deck that looked out across barrancas lush with tropical vegetation to the haze where the continent ended and the Pacific Ocean began. Laughter and bits of conversation drifted up from below, from the people gathered on the flagstone patio that surrounded the free-form swimming pool, and it occurred to her that this exact same scene had been played out in this exact same place how many dozens of times? Hundreds?

Her dad, wearing an apron her mom had bought for him during a trip to Las Vegas, the one printed to look like a tuxedo, stood next to the huge stainless steel gas grill, holding a barbecue fork in one hand and a bottle of beer in the other. He was chatting with the next-door neighbors, Barbara and Evan Norwood. Lindsey had known the Norwoods forever, had babysat their kids. Mrs. Norwood had taught her piano lessons, until, mercifully, it had become obvious to all concerned that Lindsey possessed no musical talent whatsoever.

The view, the images, the people, the smells—so little had changed. Okay, no more smell of charcoal briquettes and lighter fluid since the acquisition of the fancy gas grill, and where the portable soccer net had once straddled the place where the pool deck met lawn, a tall patio heater now stood. On the deck itself, the litter of plastic pool toys had been replaced by the large pots of flowers Mom had planted last spring.

That was my life, my childhood—soccer and swimming and babysitting and piano lessons, and Dad cooking dinner on the grill. I know I was lucky to have such a happy childhood. And I know I'm not a child any longer, but what's wrong with staying close to your parents as you get older? Isn't that the way families should be?

Should be.

But no family is perfect. Is it? And if that's true, and mine seemed to be perfect, how can that be real? What if it was all just...an illusion?

As if he'd heard her thoughts, felt her doubts, her father looked up just then and waved the beer bottle, then blew her a kiss.

She drew a shaky breath and blew him one back. That, at least, she knew was real. That her father loved her she had never doubted.

About her mother, she wasn't so sure.

Mom...did you love me? Why was there always that distance between us? You never let me get really close to you. Now I wonder...was it because there has always been another child, the little boy of your dreams—Jimmy— standing between us?

She'd been aware, growing up, of the reserve that sometimes seemed like coldness on her mother's part, but it hadn't seemed all that important then. Maybe because her dad had always been there to make up for any lack of affection, and to explain her mom's coldness in a way that had made her understand and forgive.

Now, my mother is leaving me forever, for real. And the last thing she ever does for me is to make me doubt the one thing I've always known I could count on—my dad.

A wave of resentment swept over her, but it receded quickly and when it did, it left behind the feeling she had so often these days. That awful stomach-churning feeling of a child abandoned, lost and alone.

How can I know who to trust now?

She realized, then, that she hadn't been truthful with herself or with Alan when she'd told him she wasn't doing this for herself. She *did* need to know. Or she doubted she would ever be able to believe or trust in anything again.

Down below on the patio, people were stirring, rearranging, the chatter of conversation rising with expectation and punctuated with jovial cries of greeting. Guests were arriving, the newcomers emerging through the open garage doors onto the patio, and her dad was moving to meet them, sweeping them with him into the center of the cluster of friends and neighbors already present.

Lindsey's heart gave a peculiar kick when she saw Alan come into view. It was the first time she'd seen him dressed like this—in casual clothes, jeans and light blue short-sleeved polo shirt, a navy blue windbreaker hooked on one finger and slung carelessly over one shoulder, his dark hair hidden by a Philadelphia Phillies baseball cap. But her mind insisted on flashing back to the last time she'd seen him, when he'd still been wearing his dress shirt and tie, and she felt again the smooth cotton fabric against her skin where he'd held her so closely, and smelled the scent of laundry detergent mixed with the other unknown things that made up his own particular scent. And his lips, when he'd kissed her, so unexpectedly gentle, his breath smelling faintly of coffee and peppermints. Those things—*his hand so warm on the back of my neck*—had been coming into her mind all week, and she wished to God they would stop.

Because of that, she told herself the hitch in her breathing and the quickening of her pulse wasn't for him, but for the child beside him, the little girl clinging to his arm with both hands in the shy, awkward way of ten-year-old girls meeting hordes of strangers. Chelsea Cameron was slender and tall, like her father, and wore jeans and a pink and brown windbreaker and her long dark hair was pulled up in a ponytail. Lindsey held her breath, waiting for the pang, the sense of recognition and of longing. But it had been years since she stopped seeing her baby, her precious Isabella, everywhere she went, and after a moment she relaxed and let the breath go slowly.

It was the right thing to do. I know it was. I don't regret it.

But now her mind insisted on taking her back to that time, making her remember the pain, the anger and betrayal she'd felt when her mother had taken Trent's side. Both had been furious with her for refusing to try again to get pregnant.

"Now that they know you have trouble carrying to term, they'll know what to do. They can prevent it! Don't do anything permanent, Lindsey, you don't know what medical science will come up with. They've made such advances, they're saving even tiny preemies now."

Oh, yes, Mom had had all the arguments but Lindsey had been adamant. "How can you possibly understand?" she remembered telling her mother. "You've never lost a child—you don't know what it feels like!"

The rift between them had been at its widest then, but eventually, to give her mother credit, when it came to the final separation, Susan had reluctantly accepted her decision and supported Lindsey through the trauma of the divorce. And later, no longer so self-involved and wrapped up in her own pain, Lindsey had come to realize how hard it must have been for her mother to accept the reality that she would never have grandchildren. They'd actually grown closer, it seemed, for a while.

You've never lost a child, you don't know what it feels like!

Now, the memory of those words seared her soul. Oh, God, what if it was true, the story about the little boy named Jimmy? Eyes closed, she tried to see her mother's face, the way it had been back then, tried to remember if there had been something there, some glimmer of the painful memories that were to come.

The sound of her name being called shivered the image of her mother's face like a fresh breeze across the mirrored surface of a pond. Down below on the patio, her dad was waving, calling to her. She nodded and waved back, and Alan looked up and waved, too. He spoke to Chelsea, who looked up shyly from her place close by her father's side, but didn't wave.

Here goes, Lindsey thought. She took a deep breath, pasted on a smile, and turned and went back in the house and down the stairs to join them. Her stomach was a roiling mass of butterflies, and now the only thought in her mind was: *I wonder if he'll kiss me this time.*

Chapter 5

She was prettier than I had expected, and younger.
Her hair was dark, and long. She wore it pulled back
in a ponytail, like a young girl.
Excerpt from the confession of Alexi K.
FBI Files, Restricted Access,
Declassified 2010

I wonder if I should have kissed her.

There'd been a moment there, when she'd come through the doors, emerging into the sunlight like a diva onto her stage, when it had seemed almost as though she'd expected him to. And, Alan had to admit, when he'd wanted to. Very much wanted to. The kiss he'd planted on her several days ago in the car still haunted him, burning itself into his memory at the most unexpected times, the remembered sensation becoming more intense with each replay.

Today she was wearing a sweater in a color that was

somewhere in the neighborhood of red and orange and pink and that made him think of ripe fruit, and her cheeks seemed to pick up some of that, making them more vivid than he remembered. Her eyes seemed brighter, too, shining bright blue out of that thicket of dark lashes. He didn't know what it was about those eyes—he wasn't the sort to think in literary imagery, and once again the only thing he could find to compare them to in his mind was Elizabeth Taylor. *Movie-star eyes.*

He didn't kiss her. He stepped toward her almost reflexively, but something stopped him, some inner voice warning him that it wasn't the right thing to do, at least not then. And the moment passed.

She came to him, smiling, one hand holding back her hair, although the breeze off the ocean seemed benign enough that it probably wasn't necessary. A sign of the awkwardness she was feeling, he thought. The same uncertainty he was experiencing, and which wasn't natural to him, at least not that he could recall.

"Hey, babe," he said, then wanted to chomp on his tongue. It wasn't that he'd never called a woman "babe" before, but it had never before felt so wrong. Lindsey Merrill was definitely not a "babe," which got him to wondering what kind of endearment would feel right, if their pretended relationship had happened to be real. He'd called her "honey," and "Linz," if his memory served, and none of those had felt right either.

"My daughter, Chelsea…Chelse, say hello to Lindsey," he said, more brusquely than he meant to.

Chelsea dutifully muttered, "H'lo."

"Hi, Chelsea," Lindsey said, holding out her hand. Which Chelsea didn't seem to have a clue what to do with, and Alan made a mental note to speak to her mother about maybe it being time to teach the kid some basic social graces. Covering up the awkward moment with a light touch on Chelsea's arm, Lindsey added, "I love your jacket—pink is definitely your color."

"Thank you," Chelsea said—he was glad at least for that. "My mom bought it for me."

"I hope you brought your bathing suits," Richard said, every inch the jovial host. "Hard to believe it's November, isn't it? Pool water's warm, and if it does get chilly later on, the heater over there does a pretty good job. What do you say, young lady? Feel like going for a swim? Plenty of time before we eat."

Chelsea glanced over at the pool, where several children of various ages were engaged in a game of Marco Polo, then turned a look on Alan he knew could be roughly translated as: *I'd rather have my head shaved.*

"Uh...maybe a little later?" he suggested, directing a look of appeal at Lindsey. The awkwardness of the whole thing was beginning to make his jaws ache. What had he been thinking of, to bring Chelse along on what was essentially police business?

"Of course," Lindsey was saying, and she slipped an arm around Chelsea's shoulders and scooped up her backpack. "I'm sure you'd rather get your bearings first, wouldn't you? In the meantime, how about if I show you where you can stash your stuff?"

Mutely, Chelsea nodded. Alan quelled another impulse to kiss Lindsey, this time out of sheer gratitude. He might have debated with himself whether it would be more productive to stay and chat with Richard Merrill rather than accompany the girls on their house tour, but his daughter's death grip on his arm pretty much took the matter out of his hands. So, he found himself trailing after the two of them into the house, following Lindsey's very nicely rounded bottom up a zigzagging flight of stairs.

If he'd been able to kid himself up to now about whether or not he was attracted to the lady for real, that would've put any remaining illusions to rest for good. No doubt about it, Lindsey Merrill had gotten under his skin. The only remaining question was, what was he going to do about it? It wouldn't be the first time he'd met someone in the course of an investigation that made him regret the personal and professional code of ethics that put any such liaisons off-limits. Though it might be the first time he'd doubted his ability to stick to it.

"This was my room when I was growing up." Lindsey had paused in an open doorway and turned to wait for Alan and Chelsea to join her. "Chelsea, if you like, you can leave your stuff in here. Then, if you feel like swimming, you can just come back up and change. Okay?"

"Oh, wow." This, unexpectedly, from Chelsea, who was standing in the doorway, peering into the room.

A few steps behind her, Alan's first general impression was of a whole lot of pink. Then he got close enough to get a good look. He looked at Lindsey and lifted his eyebrows.

"What can I say?" she said with a small shrug, amusement glittering in her eyes. "I'm a girl. I liked dolls."

"I'd say so." He'd moved past her, and his fascinated gaze was taking in what seemed to him like a museum of little-girlhood. Although he had to admit that, even with its very feminine pink, cream and pale green color scheme, it was in good taste, not too overwhelmingly frilly. The walls were pale green, the furniture painted cream, window curtains, bedspread and rugs all in various shades of pink. Dolls, along with a stuffed animal or two, sprawled on the bed amongst an assortment of pillows in those three colors, and filled most of the space in a rocking chair upholstered in pink, green and cream stripes. A low table in one corner of the room held a large Victorian-style dollhouse that looked both custom-made and expensive. A shelf ran all the way around the room, up high near the ceiling, and every inch of it was occupied by more dolls—most, he was pretty sure from being the father of a daughter, were Barbies. Bookshelves held books, but there were a few dolls and a couple of teddy bears tucked in here and there, as well. The only departure from the doll theme, as far as Alan could see, were the framed and matted black-and-white photographs of children playing on beaches hanging on the walls, and a collection of framed youth soccer team photos arranged above a small study desk.

"It didn't look like this when I went away to college, if that's what you're thinking," Lindsey said dryly. She was leaning against the door frame, arms folded, watching him, and her smile was crooked and unreadable. "My decorating scheme at the time was probably best described as late Springsteen-casual. My mom did this after I got pregnant and she found out I was having a girl. I was kind of amazed to discover she'd saved all this stuff."

Alan nodded, but discovered he didn't have anything to say in response. Because he knew, now, what that little bit of a smile on her face was trying to disguise. *I was having a girl.* Susan Merrill had created this room for her granddaughter, the baby who had died. Lindsey's baby.

"Careful," he said to Chelse, who was trying to peer into the open back of the dollhouse, and found his voice was filled with gravel.

Lindsey's was firm and unemotional. "No, no—she's welcome to play with anything in here. It's time someone did." To Chelsea she added with a smile, "Feel free, dear."

"Cool," said Chelsea, but she was moving on, pausing now to study the soccer team pictures. In each of them Alan noticed, a younger, slimmer, darker-haired Richard Merrill, obviously one of the coaches, stood behind or a little to one side of the double row of little girls in their team jerseys.

Chelsea leaned closer, then touched one of the photos, pointing to a slender, long-legged girl with her dark hair pulled back in a ponytail. "Is this you?"

Lindsey nodded. "That's me. We were the Red Devils. We won the championship that year."

"You were pretty." Chelsea's voice had a wistful note, and Alan felt his stomach clench.

"Geez, Chelse," he said with an uneasy laugh. "Were?"

Then he felt like a real jerk when he saw both Lindsey's and his daughter's cheeks turn pink. The latter threw him a look, a little grimace of embarrassment. "Dad, I didn't mean..."

Lindsey laughed and said, "It's okay, I know what you meant."

But Chelsea stumbled on, frowning and earnest. "I mean, you were pretty when you were a *kid*. Now, I think you're beautiful."

Oh, boy. Nice save, Chelse. Alan couldn't think of a thing to say to that, either. Then Lindsey threw him a look, and he thought the shine in her eyes might be tears. Just keeps getting better and better, he thought.

"Why," she said softly, touching Chelsea's shoulder, "what a sweet thing to say."

And while Alan watched in agonized silence, his

daughter got even pinker, then said, "I really like your hair."

"Thank you," Lindsey said, looking genuinely touched.

"I want to get mine cut," Chelsea went on, "but my mom won't let me. She says not until I'm older. And my dad says I have to do what she says." She cut her eyes at Alan, who could only lift his hands in mute wonderment. He was thinking he hadn't heard that many words come out of his daughter's mouth all at once in months.

Lindsey gave him a quick, uncertain look, as if she realized the path she now found herself on might be leading her into a place she had no business going. She cleared her throat, then said gently, "Oh, Chelsea. Your mom just doesn't want you to grow up too fast."

"But I'm already almost *ten*. I should be able to get my hair cut if I want to."

This time, Lindsey didn't even look at Alan. She reached out and touched Chelsea's hair, then let the ponytail slither through her fingers. "Trust me, you'll have lots and lots of chances to decide what you want to do with your hair. And you can also trust me when I tell you, you're probably going to regret a lot of those decisions."

"I know." Chelsea moaned, clearly unconvinced.

Lindsey smiled. "I know how you feel—I do. When I was ten, I couldn't wait to be a teenager. Then when I was thirteen, I couldn't wait to be fifteen, so I could get my learner's permit." She threw a glance at Alan, who had been unable to stifle a groan, then went on, speaking only to Chelsea, and softly, now, as if the two of them were alone in the room. Her smile had changed in some subtle way he couldn't name, but that made his throat ache anyway. "I always wanted to be…whatever was out there ahead of me.

Now, I kind of wish I'd paid more attention to how much fun it was to be ten."

Chelsea tilted her head quizzically, and didn't reply.

"What the hell was that about?"

They were on their way down the stairs, having left Chelsea in the pink, green and cream room, now thoroughly engrossed in the dollhouse.

Lindsey glanced at him in surprise. "What was *what* about?"

"You...Chelsea." He tried to make his voice light, casual. "What were you two doing, bonding?"

"I don't know what you're talking about. I was just talking to her, that's all."

"Yeah, and she was talking to you, probably more words strung together in complete sentences than she's spoken to me in a whole day, lately."

"I'm sorry. I didn't realize that was a bad thing." She spoke quietly, but her voice sounded strained. Edgy.

Ashamed of himself, Alan tried to backpedal. "It's not, just...unexpected."

He'd begun to understand that he'd wandered into territory that was unfamiliar to him; these emotional, mother-child interactions weren't something he encountered much in his line of work. He didn't know why watching Lindsey communicate with his child had stirred him so. It had seemed to come so naturally to her, and he wondered if what he felt was as simple a thing as jealousy, because lately he'd been feeling his relationship with his daughter slipping and communication a challenge, at best. Fear clutched at his belly when he thought of losing his little girl, watching her turn into an uncommunicative stranger, and after that, what next? Drugs? Everything that went with that? He'd seen too much not to know the dangers that lurked outside his protective embrace.

He wanted to say something to her, to Lindsey, to make it right, but everything he thought of seemed to bump up against the fact that she was a woman who had lost a child. He didn't know what to say to a woman under those circumstances, outside the standard phrases he was trained to use in his job, the phrases that came from habit, from a barricaded place where emotions could not encroach on the job he had to do.

I'm sorry for your loss.

He suddenly flashed on the mother of one of the victims of the weekend gang war, on her knees in the parking lot of the Whataburger, clutching her hair as if she would tear it out, and wailing at the sky. Then, on the mother of the wounded flower girl as he'd seen her in the hospital that day, still wearing her wedding clothes stained with her child's blood, her face bleached with fear, a young woman suddenly turned haggard and old.

He glanced at Lindsey, who evidently felt the look and returned it, lips set, eyes hurt and accusing. He drew breath to power an apology, but before he could deliver it, she said tightly, "You were the one who started this whole thing, pretending to be a dating couple. You were the one who wanted to come here today. Maybe you should have gone over the rules of engagement with me first."

"You're right," he said on a gusty exhalation. There was more he wanted to say but couldn't think how, there in the middle of a flight of stairs with his daughter above and her father below, and a job he'd come there to do waiting for him to get to it. "You're right. So, do you think I could have a look at those albums and yearbooks now?"

A look of vulnerability flitted across her face, and then

she tightened her lips again. "Sure. They're in the den, I think—or Dad's office, maybe. I'm not sure."

"Let's see the office first."

She felt like a traitor. Guilt and nerves made her stomach churn and her legs wobbly as she led the way down the carpeted downstairs hallway to her father's office. His private, personal space. Not that she hadn't always been welcome there; her dad had had no secrets from her, or anyone else, she was sure of that. But, she reminded herself, Alan couldn't know him as she did; he would have to find out for himself.

"In here," she said, then caught a breath and waited with pounding heart for Alan to slip past her before following him into the room.

It looked the same, smelled the same, seemed exactly as it had always been, except for the computer that now took up space on his desk, and the all-in-one printer-copier on a smaller desk set at right angles to the big one. She watched Alan take it all in from his position just inside the doorway, with his cool cop's eyes that didn't miss a thing: the desk with its rather ostentatious green leather executive's chair with brass studs the glass-front cabinet that held her dad's collection of Oriental art—an exquisite ivory Confucius he'd found at a yard sale, a jade temple jar, cloisonné bottles, a hand-painted Chinese fan, an old Chinese coin almost as big as a computer disk sitting upright on a carved rosewood stand. She'd played with them all as a child—except for the fan, which was too fragile, her dad said. Bookcases filled with an eclectic selection of books, and magazines neatly contained in wooden sleeves. The antique reproduction globe that sat on the floor beside the recliner chair where her dad sometimes napped, the pictures on the walls, signed prints of watercolors by a well-known artist who specialized in painting children and the play of sunlight and shadow. One, her favorite, of a mother sitting in a rocking chair holding a sleeping baby, he had taken down after Isabella died, and she'd known then how deeply he, too, had felt the loss of his only grandchild.

Tears stung her eyes—tears of anger and resentment rather than sadness. Anger at the circumstances that had made her bring this intruder into her father's private space, resentment of *him*, this cop, this detective, who would sniff and snoop and prod and pry, and who could never ever know her father as she knew him.

But after all, she reminded herself, she'd started this. He was only doing what she'd asked him to do.

She blinked the tears away and said abruptly, "The yearbooks are over here," as she moved past him to cross the room.

But she saw that, instead of following, Alan had paused at the desk and was opening drawers, one after the other, rifling through, then closing them again. "Doesn't lock up his desk," he commented, more to himself than to her.

She answered him anyway. "Why should he? He doesn't have anything to hide."

He had pulled out the wide center drawer. "It's been my experience," he murmured absently, "that everyone has something to hide."

Lindsey yanked a yearbook off of a shelf and turned with it clutched to her chest, biting back a new surge of anger. "You don't get it, do you? My dad is a good man. I keep telling you—" She stopped, cold clear through, as her father's voice came from just down the hallway.

"Lindsey? You guys in here? I'm putting the steaks on the grill…"

Alan slid the drawer closed without a sound and in two long strides was across the room. In the next moment, she felt his arms come around her and at the same time he turned her so that her back was against him and he was looking over her shoulder. His hands covered hers and he opened the yearbook she was holding in her hands. "Laugh..." he whispered with his lips touching her ear.

Laugh? But I can barely breathe.

It wasn't even a thought, just a feeling, maybe panic. She couldn't breathe, the air seemed to have grown too warm and thick. Her heart was pounding, so hard her chest hurt. So hard she thought he must be able to hear it.

"Laugh," he said again, a growl this time, and she managed a weak titter that was more pain than amusement.

The heat from his body was soaking into her back. She could feel his heartbeat, firm and steady, not helter-skelter, like hers. She wanted to close her eyes and lean into the heat and the heartbeat, and let the strong arms around her take over for her weakening knees. Mortified, she thought: *This is terrible. Terrible, how good it feels. Can I be so hungry for a man's touch?*

"Lindsey? Honey—"

Alan turned, unhurried, to smile at Richard Merrill as he stuck his head through the doorway. He kept his hands on Lindsey's upper arms because the way she was shaking, he wasn't sure she'd be able to stand up if he let her go. And maybe because, while professionalism had taken over his conscious mind, making it aware of every nuance of voice and expression—his own, Lindsey's, Merrill's—his body was operating on another wavelength entirely. All its senses and instincts were tuned to the woman's warm body so abruptly separated from his own, which was shrieking like a disappointed child: *No! Wait! I want...*

Meanwhile, his conscious mind was ignoring that voice and on full alert. *There—did his eyes flick, just for an instant, toward the desk? Not a trick of the light, or a nervous tick. No—he looked at the desk. I'm sure of it. Something there. Something...* The thrill of the hunt shivered through him, and goose bumps roughened his skin.

"Oops," he said, with just the slightest note of apology, "hope you don't mind. Your daughter's been showing me your old high school yearbooks. You had some sports career."

Merrill's grin was wry, his shrug self-effacing. "Very small town. I was a big frog in a little bitty puddle."

"Still. Pretty impressive. So, you played pretty much all the sports?"

"Well, the big three, anyway. Football in the fall, basketball in the winter, baseball in the spring. Everybody did. Like I said—small town. You know how it is."

"Not really," Alan said easily. "Grew up in Philly."

"Ah." Merrill nodded as if he understood.

Keeping his arm around Lindsey but holding the book in his other hand, Alan hefted it in a thoughtful way. "Must be nice, knowing everybody. Clifton. That's in...Nebraska, right?"

"Right." Merrill gestured with the tongs he was holding and seemed about to say something—most likely what he'd come there to say—but Alan interrupted.

"You still keep in touch with the gang?" *Does he seem tense? Edgy? Imagination...no. Again, no. He's definitely not comfortable with this subject.* "Go back for class reunions?"

"Wish I could." The other man's smile was regretful, sad. And, Alan had to admit, now seemed completely genuine. "I'm afraid there's not much there to go home to." His glance flicked to Lindsey. "Clifton was destroyed by a tornado in nineteen fifty-six."

Alan said, "Oh, man, that's terrible,"

And Lindsey added in a faint, shocked voice, "Daddy, you never told me about that."

Merrill gave an apologetic shrug. "I was away in college when it happened. My folks survived, thank God we had a storm cellar, but our house was destroyed. The whole town was leveled. A lot of people were killed. It was a bad time."

"Hey, man, I'm sorry," Alan said. "Surprised they didn't rebuild. What happened to everybody?"

"The town was dying anyway—you know how it is, those little midwestern towns. The young people all go off to school, find jobs in the big city. Like I did. By the time the tornado hit, half the businesses on Main Street were empty." This time the man's shrug was dismissive. "Tornado just put the town out of its misery, I guess."

"What happened to your parents?"

"Moved to Chicago. I was going to the University of Illinois in Springfield, but I transferred to the Chicago campus so I could help out. Things were tough. My dad never did really recover—died of a heart attack five years later. Mom passed away the next year."

"Sorry," Alan muttered.

Merrill waved the tongs as he turned away, with the abrupt manner of someone who finds the subject too painful to discuss. "Happens. Hey—just came to tell you two, I've put the steaks on the grill. If you like 'em rare, better get out here pretty quick. Honey—" he threw Lindsey a quick look "—I know you do, and I've got your favorite hot sauce. Son, how 'bout you?"

"Uh…same here, only hold the hot sauce. And," Alan added, "Chelsea won't eat much—she can have some of mine."

Merrill smiled and again waved the tongs, once more the genial host. "Oh, we've got hot dogs and hamburgers for the kids, if she'd rather have that." He turned to go, missing the dirty look his daughter shot at Alan as she tugged herself free of his encircling arm.

"Sure," Alan said agreeably, reeling Lindsey back into his half embrace just as her father glanced back at them, "that's fine."

There was an odd, tense moment, then while Richard Merrill paused in the doorway of his office, still smiling, clearly expecting them to leave with him, and Alan stayed planted where he was, badly wanting to stay behind and check out that middle desk drawer. And while Lindsey trembled with impotent fury, nestled close to his side.

"Hon," he said, aiming a toothy smile at her—and "hon" didn't seem any better than "babe." "You were going to show me some albums, remember?"

Lindsey's mouth popped open, but it was Richard who spoke. "Albums?"

"Yeah," Alan said, "you know—old photo albums. All the embarrassing baby pictures. She's been promising me for weeks."

Richard chuckled. "Aha—gotcha. Well, the photo albums are in the den. Lindsey knows where they are—in the big cabinet, honey, right where they've always been. But hey—if you want your steaks rare, better get on out there. Otherwise, I'm making no promises. Lindsey? You coming?"

What could Alan do but follow the man? And when they got out to the hallway, there was Chelsea, coming down the stairs, looking for him. So he had no choice but to join the group on the patio and eat and be sociable and try not to think about what might be hidden in that desk that Richard Merrill didn't want him to see.

But he was for damn sure going to get another look at the desk, first chance he got.

Lindsey made it through dinner. She wasn't sure how, because she was certain she was too upset to eat, but she knew if she didn't, Dad would surely notice and wonder what was wrong. He would notice, of course he would. Because he loved her and knew her so well.

I should never have done it. What was I thinking, to involve the police?

Recriminations played over and over in her head like a bit of song that wouldn't go away. She blamed herself more than Alan. How could she be angry with him for behaving like the cop he was? And he was in full cop mode, she could tell by the hard cold glitter of his eyes, the way they took in everything, analyzing, dissecting, scrutinizing everything. Everything about her home, her family. *My life.*

She got through the meal by concentrating on anything except her father. Anything except Alan and his sharp cop eyes. She concentrated on Chelsea, taking a lot of time making sure the little girl didn't feel self-conscious and shy and was getting acquainted with the other kids. She had a nice long conversation with Barbara Norwood, catching up with all her kids and grandkids and their various achievements at school and dance class and sports, and of course Barbara wanted to know how her dear old friend and neighbor Susan was doing, so Lindsey spent quite a bit of time filling her in on how her mother spent her days. It was a beautiful day for November, so she thought about that, and about the fact that Thanksgiving was coming up soon, and what she was going to do about dinner this year. She laughed and smiled and chewed, and around her the friendly chatter of people she'd known since childhood rose into the autumn evening like the sounds of a midsummer garden: insect hum and birdsong, water sounds and laughter. She thought about that, and what nice people they were, and how lucky—

"Lindsey?"

She jumped and spilled iced tea into her lap. Alan's hands were on her shoulders, his lips close to her ear. His hair, close-cropped as it was, tickled her cheek. "Oh, *God*, you startled me," she said, and remembered to smile. Remembered it was all for show.

"Sorry." His hands moved up and down her arms, raising goose bumps. "Getting chilly?"

"A little—dumping ice in my lap doesn't help." She was brushing vigorously at the ice chips on her pants, hoping it would disguise the bumpiness of her voice.

"Sorry," he said again, but it was obvious his mind wasn't on it.

She could hear a slight roughness in his breathing. His chin rasped her cheek like sandpaper. His breath smelled of barbecue, but not, she noticed, of beer. He was on the job; of course he wouldn't be drinking. Somehow, that fact made everything snap into focus.

"The albums," she said, her voice flat. "I suppose you want to see them now."

"Yeah, I do, if you don't mind." And she felt his lips

brush her cheek, nuzzle warm and moist into the sensitive places—her ear, her neck, her throat.

A wave of sensation rolled through her, along with a veritable tsunami of emotions, most of which were too complex to identify, just then. Anger, of course—that one she had no trouble recognizing—but anger of so many different shades and levels, it seemed there should be separate names for them all.

Chagrin, shame, frustration with herself, for experiencing desire—for that's what the sensation was, she had to be honest about it—in response to caresses that meant nothing, that were all part of a charade. A lie.

Anger with *him* for casually choosing such a cover, apparently without giving a thought to *her* feelings. *Resentment* toward him for being able to carry off the pretense without a qualm. *He* could be calm and cool, feeling—she was certain—absolutely nothing for her personally. To him she was simply a means to an end. A cover.

Humiliation at the thought that he might somehow know how his touch affected her. That could *not* happen. She made up her mind she wouldn't let it. It was all part of a job to him, one *she'd* asked him to do. For *her.*

He's doing this for me. The least I can do is try to help him.

Chapter 6

If the bodies were ever found there could be no connection with the missing couple. So, I went south. If I had not done that, if I had stayed in the north where the water was colder... But then, so many things would have been different.

Excerpt from the confession of Alexi K.
FBI Files, Restricted Access,
Declassified 2010

"What do you hope to find?" Lindsey asked. She had paused in the open sliding-glass door to look back at her father, but he was laughing and trading tales with the Norwoods, apparently oblivious to any undercurrents of betrayal and suspicion.

"Anything that might help us figure out where your mother lived before she lived here. I don't know what, exactly, but I'll know it when I see it."

She gave him a questioning look, which he thought was probably due to the note of grim frustration she heard in his voice. He couldn't blame her for wondering about him, even feeling uneasy in his company, but he couldn't muster a smile to reassure her. The truth was, he was beginning to wonder about himself, too.

It was becoming a problem, this pretense of an intimate relationship with Lindsey. And it shouldn't be. He'd started it, grabbed it as a solution to a spur-of-the-moment problem, and it shouldn't have been a big deal. He'd had occasion to use similar cover tactics before, and it had never bothered him. But this was definitely bothering him, in a lot of different ways.

Aside from a vague sense of guilt, just an itchy-twitchy feeling there was something fundamentally wrong about using a woman, a civilian in this way, the main problem was… Dammit, she was getting to him. He couldn't seem to stop thinking about her. When he wasn't with her, images of her played in a montage on continuous loop in the background of his mind. When he was with her, he wanted to be closer to her; when he was close to her, he wanted to touch her; when he was touching her, he wanted to touch her in many more intimate ways.

The truth was, he wanted to make love to her. He could see himself making love to her in all sorts of ways, ranging from the first tender, breath-stopping discoveries, to sheet-clawing, mattress-pounding, sweaty, noisy all-night sex. And no matter how much self-discipline a man might possess, it was awfully damn hard to shut down thoughts like those.

So, if she thought his manner a bit abrupt and his scowl a mite intimidating, so be it. It beat the hell out of her knowing what was really going on inside his head.

"The albums are in here," she said, and slipped past him, being particularly careful—it seemed to him—not to touch him.

As she led him through the house to the living room—or den, or whatever—he cast a frustrated look down the hallway to the door of Richard Merrill's office, which was closed now. Dammit, more than anything, he wanted—needed—to get another shot at that desk. Preferably when Lindsey wasn't around, since his invasion of her father's private space seemed to upset her. He was well-aware that any kind of unauthorized search could cause more problems than it would solve, down the road. But he knew himself. And knowing there was something there that Merrill didn't want him to see was going to be like an itch he couldn't scratch.

While Lindsey selected a couple of large and heavy-looking photo albums, Alan seated himself on the couch, leaving plenty of room on either side for her to join him. Instead, she placed the albums on the cushions, but went on standing, looking down at him, arms folded in a self-conscious way. He slid one of the albums onto his lap, then patted the empty cushion beside him and said casually, without looking at her, "Come on—sit down."

She didn't move. He heard only a small sound, and looked up to find her gazing down at him with a curious, set look on her face.

"What's the matter?"

She shook her head slightly and shifted her gaze to a spot somewhere across the room, beyond his head.

"I'm not going to touch you," he said evenly, "if that's what's worrying you."

Her eyes jerked back to him, and it seemed to him they were especially, unusually bright. He saw her throat work to produce a swallow, and his own breath thickened in his throat. The moment and the tension stretched until his eyes burned and her image began to shimmer around the edges.

He took in a sip of air. "Look—I'm going to need you to identify these for me." He managed a half smile. "Not to mention, if someone comes in, it's going to look a little odd, you standing there like a condemned prisoner in front of a sentencing judge."

She gave a little strained-sounding laugh, then reluctantly nodded. As she seated herself beside him—but maintaining a few inches distance—she ran her hands down the backs of her thighs in a way that reminded him of a little girl being careful not to wrinkle her Sunday-best dress.

He tried to concentrate on the photos, but it wasn't easy. He thought if he looked hard enough at pictures of Lindsey as a little girl it would distract him from the fact that the grown-up Lindsey was sitting right there beside him. But it didn't. Once again there seemed to be a complete disconnect between his mind, which was carefully scanning each photo, searching for the detail that would give him a clue to Susan Merrill's background, and his senses, which were wallowing in the scent of the warm, desirable woman only scant inches away, her bare arm so close to his he could feel its heat. He found himself listening for her breathing, and timing his own to hers, as if they were finding each other's rhythm in a dance. And at the same time trying not to breathe too deeply lest he inadvertently brush her arm and thus violate his promise not to touch her.

Why had he made such a stupid promise? Touching her was the one thing he wanted to do more than anything else in the world.

She reached across him suddenly, touching him in

several places at once, and his skin flinched as if she'd given him an electric shock. "There," she said, tapping one of the pictures, a square one in the style of the early nineteen seventies. "That's me playing in the snow. Big Bear, I think it was." She turned her head slightly to look into his eyes. At close range.

His head swam. He pulled back a little, frowning as he brought the rest of her face into focus, noting a little pleat of frown lines between her eyes, and the fact that her lips were slightly parted, as if she'd just drawn a sip of breath. Hungry juices pooled at the back of his throat, and his jaws creaked with the effort it took him not to give in to the desire to kiss her.

Apparently oblivious to the effect she had on him, she sat back with a sigh. "That's what I mean—Mom remembering her 'Jimmy' playing in the snow doesn't mean anything. It could just as well have been Southern California as anywhere."

He nodded, muttered something ambiguous, and turned the page. And as he did so he heard a small voice somewhere in the foggy wilderness of his mind telling him, *No—wait. There's something there. Something...* He paused, turned the page back, stared again at the photos of a chubby toddler in a pink jacket and purple mittens, dark hair sticking out in feathers from under a purple knit stocking cap, cheeks rosy with cold.

What is it? What am I missing?

But the answer eluded him, and the voice in his mind was silent. After a moment he turned the page again, with a small lingering unease that was just enough of a discomfort to make him constantly aware of it, but not quite bad enough to do something about. *Later,* he told himself. *It'll come to me.*

But a moment later, once again there was Richard Merrill's voice calling from out in the hallway. Like a diligent chaperone, Alan thought irritably, nervous about leaving him and Lindsey alone together.

Or me, alone in the house with whatever secrets he's trying to hide.

He and Lindsey both turned like guilty teenagers as her father appeared in the living-room doorway, his hands on the shoulders of a shivering and towel-wrapped Chelsea.

"Somebody here needs a ladies' room," Merrill said jovially, while Chelse, naturally, looked as if she wanted to disappear.

Alan shifted the album off his lap, but Lindsey placed her hand lightly on his shoulder as she got up. He watched her as she slipped her arm around his daughter, saying with a smile, "Oh, sure, honey, you come with me." He watched Chelse leave without a glance at him, her dad. Her eyes, as she gazed up at Lindsey, seemed almost worshipful. And again he felt it—that weird pang he couldn't identify. He wished to God he knew what it was he was feeling.

He didn't have much opportunity to dwell on it, however. Grinning and rubbing his hands together, Merrill plunked himself down in the spot recently vacated by his daughter and pulled the open album onto his lap.

"Hah—I see Lindsey's been taking you on a trip down memory lane. It's been a long time. Boy, these sure do bring back memories! Look at this—her mother and I got her that riding toy. I think it was her third birthday. It looked so darn cute in the commercials, except they left out the sound effects. Damn thing made this squeaky-squeaky sound, nearly drove us nuts." He shook his head as he stared at the old photographs, cheeks positively glowing with fatherly pride, gaze completely besotted.

And Alan thought, My God, what am I doing here?

Lindsey's right, this is nuts. The guy couldn't be any more straight arrow and genuine. Obviously a devoted husband and father. What am I doing here? Wasting my time, that's what.

By the time Lindsey and Chelsea came back, chattering together like BFFL—which his daughter had informed him meant Best Friends For Life—about things he had to assume were the latest and coolest in girl stuff because it was Greek to him, he'd all but convinced himself there was no case, cold or otherwise. Susan Merrill's "memories" were the confusion of Alzheimer's—end of story. Sad, but hey, it happened.

He was even beginning to see a bright side to this new development. If he wasn't working an investigation involving Lindsey Merrill, what was to prevent him from…well, from what, exactly, he wasn't sure. Asking her out, maybe? He wondered how she'd feel about that, and whether she'd be more receptive to the idea of making their "cover" arrangement real if he wasn't looking at her daddy as prime suspect in a very old murder.

And, he thought, *she seems to like my kid.*

That seemed to him like a good sign.

Predictably, Chelsea groaned and pouted when Alan told her it was time to go, evidently having completely forgotten how she'd groaned and pouted a few hours earlier when he'd told her where they were going to be spending the afternoon. He didn't think he was ever going to understand what made his own daughter tick, and he'd been told he could only expect it to get worse from here on in. It was a pretty depressing prospect, making him wonder if that had something to do with the stomach-twisting pangs he kept experiencing whenever he saw the rapport that was evidently developing between Chelse and Lindsey. He was beginning to feel like a clueless bystander in his own daughter's life.

While Lindsey helped Chelsea gather up her stuff and Alan tried to herd her toward the door, Richard Merrill followed along, going through the usual song and dance routine of the gracious host. Telling Chelse how glad he was she'd come, she was welcome anytime, and he hoped she'd come back again real soon. Giving Alan a good firm handshake along with a warm smile and a clap on the back and telling him the same things. Meanwhile, Lindsey stood by hugging herself, smiling nervously and looking at the ground.

And it occurred to Alan—a lightning bolt of realization, actually—that *this* was the moment. *I have to kiss her goodbye.*

Of course he would. It would be expected. It would seem odd if he didn't. Somehow, standing on her parents' doorstep in the twilight of evening, under the watchful eyes of her father and his daughter, he would have to kiss her. *And* make it look like a casual thing, something he did often and without giving it much thought. God help him.

The feeling in his belly reminded him of when he was about fourteen, getting ready for some school dance— he'd forgotten exactly which one, but it was the first time he'd actually asked a girl to go anyplace with him. He remembered walking up to Melanie Friedman's apartment door while his mom waited downstairs, and his hands being so wet with sweat he had to wipe them on his pants before he could even ring the doorbell. Remembered the butterflies in his stomach.

Terrific.

The moment was here.

"Well," he said, smiling in that awkward way, "guess I'll be seeing you…" And he still didn't have an endearment that suited her.

She nodded, her smile so stiff it made his own face hurt to look at her. He hooked an arm around her waist and pulled her in close, and after the smallest hesitation she lifted her head, and her lips were there for his taking.

So, he kissed her. And there was nothing even remotely casual about it.

He felt—heard—the faintest intake of breath, then her mouth was soft and yielding, warm against his. He felt her hand trembling slightly where it touched his waist, just above his belt, and shivers spread out from that spot and rippled across his skin.

He knew a moment of pure panic, fearing he'd lost track of time and that the kiss had already lasted much longer than it should. It should be—had to be—a brief goodbye peck, nothing more, he knew that. And yet he wanted it to go on and on, and ending it seemed the hardest thing he'd ever done.

But he did end it, somehow. Pulled back, not breathing, and then, for some reason, touched her cheek with the tips of his fingers as he whispered, "Bye…call you later, okay?"

She nodded again, and laughed—an uneven whisper of sound. Her cheek felt hot and velvety on his fingertips.

Then he was walking away from her, walking down the driveway to his car, jangled on adrenaline and the alarm going off inside his head. *Personal feelings—you're letting them cloud your judgment! Back off! Back off!*

Chelsea was quiet on the way home, as usual, and for once he didn't try to get her to talk to him. He drove with one hand over his mouth, half his mind on what he was doing, the other half lecturing himself, scolding himself for making what—for a detective—amounted to an unforgivable mistake—forgetting the Joe Friday mantra: *Just the facts, ma'am.*

That's what he had to do. Follow the facts. Investigate the facts. Wherever they might lead.

Fact: Susan Merrill remembers an act of murder and/or attempted murder committed by the man now her husband, Richard Merrill. Whether the event actually happened or not, her memory of it is fact.

Fact: There is no record of Susan Merrill's existence prior to forty years ago, in San Diego, California.

Fact: Richard Merrill's background is unverifiable.

The fact was, he was spinning his wheels, turning in circles, going nowhere. He needed answers, and there didn't seem to be any, anywhere.

Except…maybe hidden in Richard Merrill's desk?

And there was that picture, the one of Lindsey playing in the snow. What was it about that photo that bothered him? Why couldn't he put his finger on it?

It would come to him. Eventually. He hoped.

The ringing phone woke Lindsey out of a sound sleep. She reached for it, shaky, heart pounding. She was an insurance agent; a phone call in the middle of the night most likely meant disaster for someone.

She propped herself on one elbow, cleared her throat and fought to produce a professional-sounding, if somewhat husky, "Yes—this is Lindsey Merrill. How can I help you?"

She heard a soft grunt. "Well, you sound wide-awake. Don't tell me you can't sleep, either."

"Wha—who…*Alan?*" She lurched upright, shaking in

earnest now. Adrenaline, she told herself. His voice was unexpected at that hour of the night. Woken out of a sound sleep—who *wouldn't* be startled?

"Yeah, it's me. Sorry to wake you."

"No problem," she murmured, and put one hand over her eyes, gritting her teeth as she tried to slow her breathing. "What—"

"Couldn't sleep." His voice was brusque, all business. She could imagine his eyes, hard and cold as flint. Cop eyes. "Hey, listen—I've got a question for you."

"Yeah, okay." She cleared her throat; her heart rate seemed to be returning to normal. "Sure, go ahead."

"Did you ever own a snowsuit?"

She laughed, and said, "I beg your pardon?" Whatever she might have expected, it wasn't this.

"A snowsuit—you know, one piece, zipper down the front, mittens on a string threaded through the sleeves so you won't lose 'em. Oh, and a hood that cinches up tight around your face…your mom and dad ever make you wear something like that?"

"Uh…no, I don't think so. Why would they? This is San Diego!"

"Even when you went to the mountains to play in the snow?"

"No! We went like…once, that I can remember. Why would they buy me a snowsuit to play in the snow once? You saw the pictures. I was wearing a regular jacket. And I think I had on a knitted cap and mittens—they probably bought me those just for the occasion. Why on earth would you ask such a thing?"

"Think about it." His voice was rough, gravelly. An involuntary shiver ran down her spine.

She gave a helpless shrug. "I…can't. I don't know what—"

"Your mom—when she told you about Jimmy playing in the snow. You said she mentioned a snowsuit. Remember that? Are you sure—are you *positive* that's what she said? She specifically said he wore a snowsuit?"

"Yes…yes, I'm sure she said *snowsuit*." She caught a quick breath, feeling in short supply, suddenly. "She said he looked like—"

"—a penguin. That's what I thought." There was a long exhalation. "Okay, well, that field of haystacks we're looking in just got a whole lot smaller."

"I still don't—"

"Lindsey, I grew up in Philadelphia. I remember snowsuits. I wore snowsuits. Hot—so many layers underneath you couldn't move, and God help you if you had to pee or scratch an itch. Every kid who grew up where it's cold had to wear snowsuits. Like you said—people who live where it's warm don't buy snowsuits just to go play in the snow once in a blue moon."

"So, that means…"

"You're obviously not awake yet. It means your mother remembers living someplace where there was snow in the winter—on a regular basis."

Lindsey drew her knees up and wrapped her arms around them, and felt steadier. "That narrows it down some, I suppose," she said doubtfully.

"More than you realize, actually. Remember what your mom said about floating? I think she was on a boat. Which means not only was it someplace cold in the winter, but it had to be near water. So, I'm thinking, the Atlantic Ocean or the Great Lakes. Anyway, it gives me a place to start. But in the meantime, Lindsey…I need a favor."

"Um…" She cleared her throat, listened to her hammering heart, and then herself saying, "Sure."

"I need to get back in your parents' house. When your father isn't home. Can you do that for me?"

Lindsey couldn't answer him. Her stomach felt hollow, and she was cold.

After listening to her silence for several seconds, Alan said in a soft-gruff voice, "Look…Lindsey. I know how you feel—I do. Please believe me when I tell you, I'm not trying to railroad your dad. I'm not accusing him of anything. I'm just trying to find out what happened to your mom that she's having these terrible memories. It could very well be that she's mistaken about who shot her—if anyone shot her. It could be your dad is guilty of nothing more than trying to protect her. Be that as it may, there is something in that desk of his he's nervous about. Maybe it's nothing more than his personal diary, or…I don't know, his secret stash of…whatever. But I really need to find out what it is he doesn't want me to see. Okay?"

He waited, and she still couldn't answer. After a moment she heard him sigh. "Okay, look. If you don't want to do this, just tell me now. Tell me you've changed your mind about wanting to find out whether there's any truth to your mother's nightmares, and I'll back off right now. Is that what you want?"

Yes! Oh, yes—I wish I'd never brought this to you. I don't want to know! Her heart cried out in anguish, but she knew it was lying. The genie was out of the bottle, and there was no putting it back.

She put her hand back over her eyes and, after unsticking her tongue from the roof of her mouth, managed to croak, "No. No, it's okay. I'll…um. Okay. He golfs with Mr. Norwood, our—the next-door neighbor. On Mondays."

"What time?"

"I don't know—mornings, I think. No, wait—yes, it's mornings, and they usually have lunch together afterward. So, anytime before noon should be good." She pressed her fist tightly against her chest. "Let me know what time you want to go and I can meet you there."

Waiting tensely, she heard a long exhalation. "Okay, good. I'll call you Monday morning once I know what my day's going to look like. And Lindsey…thanks…I know this isn't easy."

She didn't know what she replied. All she wanted was for him to be gone so she could curl herself up in a ball underneath the covers and give in to the ache in her throat, her chest, her entire body. But once the connection had been broken, instead she went on sitting with the lifeless phone in her hand, listening to the far-off shushing of waves against the rocks below the cliffs.

After a while she laid the phone back on the nightstand and unfolded herself, stiff as an old woman. She got out of bed and went to the bathroom, where she washed her face with cold water. As she patted herself dry, she stared at herself in the mirror, noticing the shadows under her eyes…the lines around her mouth she'd swear hadn't been there before.

Oh, God…what have I done? Mom's illness is tearing our family apart, and now I have to destroy everything that's left? And, as if that weren't enough, I have to go and develop some kind of…something—a crush? Lord knows what this is, because it can't possibly be love!—*for the man who is the instrument of my family's destruction? How* could *I?*

And please God, tell me…how can I stop it?

She didn't know how long she stood in front of the

mirror, gazing into her own anguished eyes, before she felt it—the slow relaxing of tension in her body, the easing of the muscles around her mouth and eyes. A quietness came over her…a sense of something like peace—or acceptance, perhaps.

Because, she thought, whatever else happens, I know Dad loves me, and I know he loves Mom.

It doesn't matter if I take Alan to the house, and it doesn't matter if he searches Dad's desk. He won't find anything. Because my dad has nothing to hide.

Alan stared down at the square of unfinished wood, not wanting to believe, not wanting to accept what lay there before him.

"I don't understand." Lindsey spoke in the voice of a bewildered child, and he refused to hear the pain in it. Frustration vibrated through his insides and fury burned behind his eyes.

Too late, dammit. Too late!

"It was here," he said flatly. "You can see it yourself." He pointed to the dark rectangle of glue residue about half an inch wide, framing a space the exact size of a standard manila envelope. He gave the brush in his hand another twitch, and a few more grains of fine black powder sifted down onto the bare wood surface. "Something was taped to the bottom of this drawer—with masking tape, probably. But it's gone now." He exhaled slowly through his nose and reeled in his disappointment, allowing himself only a whispered, "Damn."

"It could have been anything," Lindsey said, her voice now unsteady but defiant. She was hugging herself, he saw when he glanced at her. Had the shakes, probably.

"Yes, it could. Anything at all. And whatever it was, your father couldn't take even the remotest chance that a police homicide detective might get his hands on it."

"You don't know that!" It was a cry of pain, as if he'd wounded her. "You can't possibly know when—" She froze.

An instant later, so did he. They'd both heard it—the sound of a car pulling into the driveway. The creaking of a garage door rising.

"I thought you said—"

"It's too early! Something must have—it's not even noon!" Her eyes were huge above the hands clamped across her mouth. She moved them long enough to whisper hoarsely, "Oh, God—what am I going to do?"

"Go—now. Stall him. I'll get this cleaned up. Tell him— hell, never mind. Tell him anything. *Just stall him.*"

She nodded and went, leaving the office door partly open. He had to admire her for that presence of mind, since the sound of the door closing and then reopening would have given him away for sure.

He moved quickly, sliding the drawer back into place with as little noise as possible, then putting everything back in it, careful to put things exactly as he'd found them. Knowing that, if Merrill was as knowledgeable as he appeared to be, he'd have left some kind of "tell" that would let him know instantly that someone had violated his secret hiding place. Couldn't be helped.

As he worked, he followed Lindsey's progress with his ears, listening to the sound of the kitchen door opening, a brief snatch of conversation:

"Dad—you're home early! What happened—"

"Lindsey? What are you doing here at this time of day, honey? Is that Alan's—"

Before the door closed, cutting off the rest.

God help us, he thought. *I just hope she can stall him long enough.*

Chapter 7

*The woman talked a lot. She told me about her
child, a little boy, how much she loved him, and how
much he needed her. I knew what she was trying to
do. She was trying to make me see her as a human
being, a mother with a child. Hoping to soften my
heart, I think. But I had a job to do. You must understand—they were not human beings to me. Simply
objects to be disposed of.*

*The man, though...the man was very quiet. He
barely spoke, but his silence didn't reassure me. I
could hear determination in that silence.*

Excerpt from the confession of Alexi K.
FBI Files, Restricted Access,
Declassified 2010

"I thought you'd be home," Lindsey said with a nervous
laugh. "We, uh..."

"You know Ev and I always play golf on Mondays." Her

father's lips were tight, his eyes narrowed with suspicion, and there was a coldness in them she'd never seen there before. "So, where *is* Alan?" His eyes darted to one side, aimed past her at the door she'd just come through.

Choosing to ignore the question, Lindsey shifted slightly, trying to block his path, saying brightly, "Oh—gosh, Daddy, I forgot about your golf date. Wait—that's right—this is Monday, isn't it? But don't you usually have lunch together?" And oh, it felt so wrong. So awful. "Is everything okay? Is Ev—"

"Everything's fine. Ev's fine—just had an appointment with his chiropractor. Took a rain check on lunch. Alan inside? I'd like to say hello to him, since he's here." He threw her a crooked smile as he reached past her to open the door, but she couldn't help but notice the smile didn't reach his eyes.

She squeezed back against the door frame as he brushed past her, then followed him into the kitchen, breathless, her heart pounding in her belly, fear squeezing her insides. "Dad—wait—please let me explain…"

He paused a moment to look at her, and the hurt in his face felt worse than a slap. "Honey, you're a grown woman. Why do you feel you need to explain?"

She opened her mouth to reply—with what, she didn't know—but he was moving past her again, striding purposefully through the kitchen and into the hallway. All she could do was follow, while her heart seemed bent on pummeling its way out of her chest.

In the hallway she nearly slammed into her father, who had stopped dead in the middle of it. Looking past him, she saw Alan standing at the top of the stairs. He was shirtless, and drying his dripping wet hair with a towel.

Air gusted from her lungs. She managed to gasp out,

"This isn't what it looks like, Dad." She felt an absurd impulse to giggle.

He turned his head to look at her, his expression quizzical. "Honey, like I said, you're a grown woman. The only thing I can't quite understand, is why *here?* Don't the two of you have your own places?"

Now she did laugh. A nervous and guilty titter that almost eclipsed Alan's, "Oh—good to see you, sir. Just stopped by—"

"To pick up the dollhouse," She finished, then stopped, fingertips pressed to her lips.

Where had that come from? She had no idea. She was shocked, shaking inside, and at the same time felt absurdly pleased with herself—quite exhilarated. Realizing the two men were both staring at her in what appeared to be uncomprehending silence, she rushed on.

"Daddy, I didn't want you to know I was giving away your dollhouse. I didn't want you to think... I'm sorry, Daddy, I know you made it for me, and I love it, but it's just been sitting there." When had she become such a good liar? And yet, it was perfect, so perfect she wondered if the idea had been there in her subconscious all along. "And Chelsea enjoyed it so, and I just thought..."

"No, no, no—honey, it's perfectly all right." Her dad's voice sounded relieved, and his arms were around her, gathering her into his familiar embrace. She buried her face in his shoulder and breathed in the familiar smells of Bay Rum and Tide detergent and the faintest hint of the single beer he'd probably enjoyed with Evan Norwood in lieu of lunch. "I made that dollhouse for you, honey, it's yours to do with as you please. And although I'd always hoped I'd live to see my grandkids enjoy it, if you want to give it to a little girl who will love it and play with it the way you used to, that's okay with me."

Lindsey lifted her head from his shoulder. Through a tear shimmer she could see Alan at the top of the stairs, absently mopping water droplets from his chest and staring down at her with a bemused look on his face. She drew a breath and sniffed. "Daddy, are you sure?"

"Absolutely." He gave her a little shake as he moved her to arm's length and said severely, "And you should know that about your dad. Now, you go and gather up all the little pieces, and I'll give Alan a hand carrying that monster down the stairs."

She nodded, only half paying attention. Now that the crisis appeared to have passed and disaster averted, she couldn't seem to take her eyes off the spectacle of Alan, naked to the waist. She couldn't help but notice he was pretty impressive, even for Southern California, land of compulsive joggers and workout addicts.

"Hope it was okay, my borrowing your bathroom." Alan's voice, speaking to her father as he climbed toward him up the stairs, brought her to her senses. She closed her mouth and cleared her throat self-consciously as he went on, "I've been at a crime scene all morning. You know... didn't feel good about touching anything until I'd washed up a bit."

He smiled crookedly, and Lindsey watched her father clap him on the shoulder and say warmly, "Son, that's quite all right. You're welcome here anytime."

"Just give me a minute to get my shirt on. I sure do appreciate this. Chelsea is going to go nuts when she sees that dollhouse. It's awfully kind of you and Lindsey—not to mention generous...."

The voices trailed off as the two men disappeared into

the upstairs hallway, and Lindsey was left, as she seemed to be so often these days, with a childish urge to cry. She was turning into an emotional wreck, she thought, always feeling like a little girl, sick to her stomach at the thought of disappointing her daddy. Something about having her belief in her parents shaken, she supposed. Particularly a parent who had always been the rock she'd depended on, the pillar of strength, security and stability in her life.

"Oh, grow up, Lindsey," she muttered to herself as she almost ran up the stairs in her dad's wake. When she reached the top she could hear the two men talking farther down, somewhere in the vicinity of the bathroom. From the sound of things, it appeared Alan was showing Dad his weapon.

Perfect—bonding over guns. Guy stuff.

Anger came almost as a relief. She made a disgusted sound and stormed into her old room, where she blew off steam gathering up the dolls and accessories that went with the dollhouse and packing them into a beach bag she found in her old closet. She didn't even look at the two men when they came in to pick up the unwieldy dollhouse, laughing together and conversing in monosyllables the way men do when they're involved in a task requiring joint effort. But she was seething. She wanted to scream at Alan: *How dare you "bond" with my dad! How can you pretend to be his friend when you suspect him of being some kind of monster? A murderer?* Liar!

But she kept her face averted so they wouldn't see the anger.

She went down the stairs ahead of the house movers. By the time they had the dollhouse wrestled into the back of Alan's SUV, she had herself under control and was able to give her dad his usual goodbye kiss on the cheek. He hugged her and shook Alan's hand, then waved them off and went back in the house.

Watching him go, Lindsey thought he looked older, suddenly. Old and...unbearably lonely.

Alan opened the driver's side door of his SUV and took out his jacket, gave it a shake before shrugging into it and adjusting it over the holstered weapon at his hip. Once more fully clad, he looked at Lindsey and said quietly, "You don't have to do this. I can take the dollhouse to your place—I guess you can leave it there, can't you?"

She shook her head. Her chest felt tight, and her voice showed it. "I want Chelsea to have it. It's time somebody played with it. It deserves to be played with."

He ran a hand through his hair and blew out a breath with a little gust of laughter. "Well, I'm sure it will be. And I have to say, it was a brilliant idea. I'm impressed."

"It was a lot better than yours," she said hotly. "What was that business with the towel? No shirt? Please."

At least he had the grace to look a *tiny* bit embarrassed. "Yeah, well...it was the best I could come up with on the spur of the moment."

She snorted. "You know, you do seem to have a certain lack of imagination in these circumstances. How come all of your 'spur of the moment' ideas seem to involve sex?"

He burst out laughing, and said with an unexpectedly endearing shrug, "Hey, I'm a guy, what can I say?"

And somehow she discovered that her anger had evaporated, and now she couldn't help but smile. For a long moment she just looked at him, and he looked back at her. Words they'd both spoken—*guy...towel...no shirt... brilliant...sex*—now seemed to echo back at her, filling her mind with the accompanying images, and she had no doubt whatsoever that the same montage was playing in *his* mind. His eyes…she remembered wishing they'd look at her with warmth, the way they'd looked at her mother. But *this*—this wasn't warmth, this was *heat*. And it made her feel breathless. Like opening the door of a roaring furnace.

She wondered if she might have made a sound—an involuntary gasp, perhaps—because Alan gave a slight start and said abruptly, "Better be going. I'll start looking into cold cases, now that we have an idea where to start. I'll let you know if I find anything that looks promising."

He was about to get into his car. She said, through stiff lips, "Better kiss me goodbye. Dad's probably watching."

He nodded—grimly, as if faced with an unpleasant task. She stepped closer, steeling herself. He reached out and hooked his hand around the back of her neck, pulled her to him and kissed her, roughly and hard.

She felt the firm and vibrant shape of his mouth, the faint rasp of his half-day's beard, the strength of his hand on her neck, but before any of that could fully register in her consciousness, he took his mouth away from hers, exhaled sharply and wrapped both arms around her and pulled her close. He held her that way, as if they'd both just come through a terrifying moment together, and she felt his heart thumping against her chest and realized her arms had gone around him, and that she didn't want to let him go. He held her for a long time, and it seemed to her he didn't want to let her go, either.

But he did. He drew back with a soft laugh of apology, and a breathy, "Well…"

She drew back, too, and managed to laugh, a little. "Um…" she said, and then, "yeah."

"So…okay, then. I'll call you." He got in his car, closed the door, started up the motor and drove away.

Unsteadily, she walked to her car, paused to wave at the house, knowing that behind those silent windows her dad would be watching. She got in, started up the motor, and drove away, following the route back to her office on autopilot, while somewhere in the back of her mind a voice, like a little yippy dog, was barking, *Wait! Wait! What just happened? Are you just going to ignore it? Hey!*

In firm and determined voice, she answered herself: *I can't think about this now. I…will…not…think…about it.*

The Homicide Unit was enjoying a relatively calm period, in the wake of the flare-up of gang violence the previous week. Alan spent Monday afternoon following up leads in a couple of open cases and trying not to think about the very large dollhouse sitting in the back of his SUV. And having considerably better luck with that than not thinking about the woman who'd put it there. And particularly about what had happened right after they'd put it there.

So, what, exactly, did happen? You kissed her—big deal. You've kissed her before, a couple of times—so what? It was part of the cover story. Part of the job.

Yeah, true…but it wasn't even the kissing that bothered him so much, as what had happened after *that*. Kissing her had been necessary, maybe, for their cover, but not the holding. He didn't even know where it had come from, that sudden need to hold her. And then, to find it so hard to let her go…and hours later to still be feeling the shape of her in his arms, her warm body melting into his, her heart thumping against his ribs, her hair sleek and soft on his cheek. To find it so hard to stop thinking about how good it had felt, and how sweet she smelled…

He told himself it was only his libido talking, that it had just been too long since he'd enjoyed the company of a warm and willing woman. Except that, when he thought about calling up one of several ladies he knew would be more than happy to fill his need for female companionship, no strings attached, he found the idea somewhat less than appealing. Not worth the effort.

With the leads on his open homicides exhausted, he got himself a prepackaged ham and cheese sub and some fairly decent coffee from the cafeteria and went back to his desk. Day shift was just signing off, so he spent some time waving off several invitations to join the usual crowd at the usual after-shift watering hole before settling down to his search. He started looking in the Chicago area, figuring that was where Richard Merrill had supposedly gone to college following the demise of his alleged hometown, so it was as good a haystack to start with as any other. He found a couple of cold homicides involving male gunshot victims of roughly the right age range whose bodies had been found in bodies of water—one river, one Lake Michigan—that might bear further investigation. He'd also discovered that records from the 1960s weren't that easy to access. He shut down his computer somewhere around ten o'clock, talked himself out of calling Lindsey to tell her what he'd found—or hadn't found—and went home to bed.

On Tuesday, Alan's partner, Carl Taketa, returned from a two-week leave of absence, during which he and his long-time girlfriend, Alicia Alvarez from the Crime Prevention and Education department, had made a brief stop at city hall to tie the knot—without advance notice to anyone in homicide, except the captain, of course. After which they'd hopped a plane to Cancún for their honeymoon. Having spent a mostly sleepless night trying not to think about Lindsey Merrill naked and sharing his bed, Alan was pretty sour on the subject of weddings, honeymoons and happily-ever-afters in general. He gave Carl about five minutes to enjoy the good-natured ribbing, congratulations and back-slappings from other members of the unit before hustling him off to a shooting at a convenience store out in the North Park district.

"Hear you had some excitement while I was gone," Carl said as they were en route to the scene.

Alan was driving—at a sedate pace, since the victim, a would-be robber, wasn't going anywhere, and the shooter, the elderly Vietnamese owner of the convenience store, was reportedly sitting quietly in the company of uniformed officers and it didn't seem likely he'd be going anywhere, either.

"Yeah," he said, and for a moment had to think what excitement his partner was referring to. "A bit."

He could feel Taketa looking at him. After a moment, Carl shifted awkwardly and said, "Sorry about not telling you. About getting married, you know? It was the way Alicia wanted it. Not a lot of fuss. You know if we'd had the big deal, you'd have been my best man."

"No, no, that's okay, I understand." To be truthful, Alan hadn't even thought about that aspect of his partner's elopement, and in retrospect could only feel profound relief he'd managed to escape the whole best man, bachelor party, reception-toast thing. He threw him a glance and then added dryly, "I'd just like to know how you managed to keep it a secret, the way news travels in the house."

"I'm kind of surprised about that myself." Again, Alan felt the man's eyes on him, and after a moment Taketa said, "Speaking of news, word is you caught yourself a cold case."

Alan snorted. "*Possible* cold case. You been talking to the captain?"

Carl grinned. "He mighta mentioned it. So, this woman who brought you the story. She's hot, right?"

Hot? The term took Alan by surprise. He tried now to think if it suited Lindsey Merrill, and decided, to his own puzzlement, that it didn't, no more than "babe" and "hon" did. Not that she wasn't attractive—of course she was. Her body—fit and trim, but soft and round where it needed to be—certainly qualified as "hot," though the way she carried herself was in no way overtly sexy. Except for those Hollywood eyes, her features were unremarkable, but when he thought about how her mouth had felt against his...well. Best not think about that just now. Although... she did have nice skin... Her hair? That, too, although attractively cut and styled, wasn't exactly the kind of mane poets rhapsodized about.

No, taken as a whole, Lindsey had too much class—or something—to be thought of as "hot." In fact, the woman seemed to defy his every attempt to label or categorize her. That, in itself, was suggestive of something, although he couldn't define that, either.

Unable to come up with a reply to Carl's question, he settled for, "Okay, tell me how that's relevant."

"Hah. Woman comes to you, tells you her mother—who has Alzheimer's, mind you—now believes her husband killed her real husband and tried to kill her. But she doesn't know when or where this happened. And you take on the case. Way I see it, the woman has to be a hottie."

Alan muttered a frustrated and sibilant obscenity under his breath.

"Okay, tell me you'd have paid any attention to the woman's story if she'd been old or ugly."

Alan snorted again but didn't bother to reply.

"Hey," Carl said with a shrug as he turned in his seat to face front again, "doesn't matter. I'm your partner, you know I'll help any way I can. We get this shooting wrapped up, run it all by me. Maybe we can come up with something."

Alan shot him a look. He felt genuinely grateful, and was thinking how glad he was to have Carl back riding shotgun again. But it wasn't the kind of thing he was inclined to voice out loud, so he didn't.

After a long pause, Carl said, "Speaking of hotties, you given any thought to…you know. Getting back on the horse?"

Jolted, Alan flashed Carl another look and tried to make light of it. "So, what is this, you take the plunge, now you want to pull everybody into the pool along with you? Misery loves company, is that it?"

"More like happiness does." Carl sounded dead serious. "No, I mean it, man. There's no better way to live than a good marriage."

"And no worse way than a bad one," Alan said dryly. "Been there…done that."

Carl shrugged. "So, you've learned a thing or two, you'll get it right next time."

"You know the odds are against that, right? For cops, especially? You and Alicia—at least she's on the job, too, so she knows what she's getting into."

"True, that helps, sure it does. But it's not a requirement. There are others…"

His voice trailed off, and Alan didn't bother to fill in the blanks. They both knew from personal experience the truth of the statistics involving marriages among members of law enforcement.

After a moment, though, Carl said, "So, the hottie—what does she do?"

Alan let out an exasperated breath. Taketa was a bulldog once he got his teeth into something, so there wasn't much hope of getting him off the subject. "Sells insurance," he said shortly. "Has her own agency."

Carl was nodding. "Good...good. Financially independent is always good. Has a life of her own—means she probably wouldn't be emotionally dependent on you, the way your ex was."

"Once again...irrelevant." Alan made sure his tone was firm...unequivocal—not that it would make any difference to Carl. "No way I'm pursuing this, the woman is part of an ongoing investigation."

"True," Carl said, nodding, "but after?"

Alan gave the windshield a wry and humorless grin. "Yeah, I'm sure she's going to feel all warm and fuzzy towards the cop who put her beloved daddy away for murder."

After a thoughtful silence, Carl said, "You really feel that's the way it's gonna go down?"

It was Alan's turn to shrug. "Gut feeling, that's all I've got. And I mean, *all*. There's something off about this guy, Merrill, but I can't put my finger on it. And, I've got nothing to go on except the memories of an Alzheimer's patient about something that supposedly happened over forty years ago, God only knows where. What does that make me—crazy, right?"

He could hear the grin in his partner's reply. "Told

you—it's hormones, that's all. Can't be denied." There was a pause, and then: "Does she know about Chelsea?"

"Who?" Alan said, although he knew very well who.

"The hottie."

Resigned, he said noncommittally, "She's met her."

"And?"

Alan exhaled and muttered glumly, "She gave her a dollhouse. *Her* dollhouse."

Carl let out a hoot of laughter, just as they pulled up in front of the convenience store. Then, as Alan rolled the sedan to a stop, they both sat for a moment in silence, gazing at the small Asian gentleman sitting slumped and lost-looking in the open doorway of a patrol car.

Carl sighed. "Please tell me we aren't going to have to arrest this poor guy for defending his business against some scumbag that tried to rob him?"

Alan looked at him and opened his car door. "We just follow the facts," he said.

"I think we're going at this all wrong," Carl said. He leaned his chair back, propped one foot on Alan's desktop and laced his fingers together behind his head—for a moment, until Alan gave him a look. Then he quickly shoved himself upright and leaned forward. "I mean, we've been looking at it from the perspective of a homicide case."

"Which, if we assume Susan Merrill's memories are accurate, it is," Alan said with a half-stifled yawn. "Taking her recollections as facts—which is already a stretch—we have a couple, husband and wife, probably in their mid-to-late twenties. Both shot, most likely on board a boat of some kind. Problem is, we don't know where, what kind of boat, what body of water. Could have been just about anything, anywhere."

It was late Friday evening, long past the time when a newly married man should have been home with his bride, but Alicia was enjoying a night out with her mom and sister—dinner and a chick movie, Carl had told him—so Alan's conscience was clear. Alan had spent most of Thursday and Friday in court, testifying, and this was the first chance he'd had to get together with his partner and brainstorm the Merrill case—if he could call it that.

He picked up his mug, drained the last mouthful of cold coffee and made a face as he set the mug back down. "Truth is, I don't know where to start. Rather—I did start, with the Chicago area, which is where Merrill supposedly went to college. Where do I go from here—that's the question."

"Uh-uh." Carl was shaking his head. "That's what I mean. You've been looking at this like a homicide case. But this woman—Susan Merrill—she *survived*."

"Her husband didn't. *If* what she says is true."

"Yeah—*if*. That's speculation. But we know for sure Susan survived *something*. Right? You've gotta figure her memories are real, or we wouldn't even be talking about it. So, she gets shot—or injured in some way—didn't you say she's got a scar on the side of her head?"

"According to her daughter."

"Okay, so, say she's shot, the bullet grazes her, she goes into the water. She remembers floating, right?"

"Right…" Alan said, frowning. He was getting a prickly sensation under his skin, because he was beginning to see what his partner was getting at. He sat up straighter.

"Seems to me," Carl went on, "it would have taken some

kind of miracle for this woman, gunshot wound to the head, in the water—"

"At night," Alan interjected.

Carl nodded agreement. "To have *somehow* survived. For one thing, that water couldn't have been *too* cold, or hypothermia would have finished her for sure. Which lets out the Great Lakes, and probably the North Atlantic coast, and for sure the whole Pacific coast, which is cold as a—"

"Which leaves the Gulf of Mexico or the Southeast coast." Alan shook his head irritably. "But the snowsuit—"

"Forget the snowsuit. All that means is the woman lived somewhere cold when her kid was little. Doesn't mean that's where the crime took place."

"Okay," Alan said. He took a breath and let it out. "Okay." He was tingling all over, now. He swiveled toward his computer screen. "So, somebody must have picked this woman up—fishing boat, maybe. Somebody's yacht. Point is, whoever found her, it would have been a pretty big deal…"

"Newsworthy," Carl said, grinning. "Film at eleven." He spun his chair around and pulled out his keyboard. "What year did you say this was?"

Two days later. Early Sunday afternoon. Alan and Carl sat hunched in front of their respective computer monitors, staring at the image on both screens.

"So," Carl said, "what do you think? Is it her, or not?"

For a moment Alan didn't answer. The image—a small, murky, black-and-white newspaper photo of a woman's face—reminded him too acutely of the digital photos of homicide victims they often snapped at the crime scene and then thrust in front of potential suspects or witnesses along with the words, "Do you know this woman?" The face was puffy, the eyes half-open, and a bandage obscured the left side of her head, including part of her face. It could be anybody, he thought.

"I dunno," he muttered. "Maybe." He switched back to the article from the *Richmond Times-Dispatch*, dated the fifth of September, 1969. It hadn't made the front page; Ho Chi Minh had died a few days previously, and William Calley had just been charged in the My Lai Massacre, so the woman rescued from the Chesapeake Bay by two blue crab fishermen only made page two. The photo bore the inevitable caption: *Do You Know This Woman?* The article alongside the photo was headlined MYSTERY WOMAN PULLED FROM BAY IN MIRACLE RESCUE.

> *An unidentified woman, believed to be in her late twenties or early thirties, was found barely alive and floating in the Chesapeake Bay early Wednesday afternoon, rescued by two sharp-eyed fishermen, Ed and Patrick Paulsen. The brothers from Reedville, Virginia, were heading home after a day of fishing for blue crab when they spotted the woman, who was partially tangled in some floating debris. It is believed the debris, probably washed into the Bay by last week's heavy rains, remnants of Hurricane Camille, may have helped save the woman's life.*
>
> *"It was just a miracle we even seen her," said Ed Paulsen. "We thought first it was just a pile of reeds and driftwood and stuff. Then I seen something move."*

The Paulsen brothers are being hailed as heroes today, but according to Patrick, "I guess we was just in the right place at the right time."

The woman, who is suffering from a head injury as well as exposure, was taken to a hospital in Richmond where she is reported to be in serious but stable condition. Anyone with information regarding this woman is urged to contact authorities immediately.

Chapter 8

The night was especially fine. The air was soft and warm—I recall thinking it was a night for lovers. The moon hadn't yet risen—I had planned for that—and the stars were brilliant. I had lived in the city for so long I had forgotten about stars. Then, just before dawn, the fog came. It seemed like an omen. I knew the time had come.
Excerpt from the confession of Alexi K.
FBI Files, Restricted Access,
Declassified 2010

"Sure sounds right," Carl said. "Even to the head injury. Just wish the picture was better."

"I'll contact Richmond PD, see if they can send us a better one." Alan shoved back from the computer and swiveled to face his partner. "Then I'll have to see if Lindsey can ID the woman—her memories of her mother go back a lot further than mine do. But even if this is Susan Merrill, all it tells us is how she survived. Doesn't tell us how she got into the Chesapeake, or whether the man calling himself Richard Merrill had anything to do with putting her there."

Carl didn't reply. He was staring at his computer screen, eyes squinted in concentration. Alan knew that look. "What are you thinking?" he asked.

After another two beats of silence, Carl flicked him a glance along one shoulder. "What am I thinking? Looking at the map…seems to me the Chesapeake is right handy to a whole lot of the northeast, including some major population centers. Like Baltimore…D.C.—" he tapped the screen "—your old stomping grounds—Philadelphia, right? Some of these might even be snowsuit territory, you know?"

Alan heaved a sigh. "Yeah, I guess it does narrow the search area. Should make it a little easier. Maybe."

"It'd make it even easier if we had help." Carl's eyes glittered, giving him a crafty look.

"What are you suggesting?" Alan asked, warily this time.

Carl spun around and held up a hand. "Look, I know what you're going to say, but hear me out, okay? I know you and your old man—"

"Stop right there."

"No—wait a minute. Like I said—hear me out. I know you and your dad don't see eye to eye—"

"Don't see eye to eye? How's about, we haven't spoken in twenty years."

"—and that you blame him for your mom's sui-cide—"

Alan grunted, but didn't voice the thought that popped into his mind: *Better than blaming myself.* That was the trouble with long, boring stakeouts with his partner, he thought. Entirely too much opportunity for soul-baring conversation.

"—and I get that you don't want to call on the man now when you need help. But he was on the job back then when this happened, and he's got buddies—fellow cops—who were, too. They'd all be retired now, obviously, but the ones that're still alive, I'll bet you anything they stay in touch. Housewives and back fences got nothing on retired cops when it comes to spreading gossip and inside information. This was an unsolved case, and I'll bet you anything there's at least one retired cop out there who still remembers it. Probably wakes him up at night every now and then, gnawing at him, because maybe it's the one case he couldn't close." Carl paused, and Alan gazed back at him and didn't comment, because half-forgotten names and faces were scrolling through his mind. After a moment, Carl gave him a little smile and said, "And I'll bet you've got somebody in mind, right now. Am I right?"

Walter "Buck" Busczkowski. His dad's old partner and Alan's unofficial godfather, the closest thing he'd had, back then, to a functioning parent. A tough ex-marine and Vietnam vet, who'd showed him the escape route from the dead-end road his own life had seemed to be taking….

Alan snorted and reached for his phone. Then put it back and picked up the computer mouse instead. Twenty years was too long to trust his memory of the return address from an old Christmas card.

The call blindsided him. It came on Tuesday morning, through the department switchboard. He'd given Buck Busczkowski his private cell number, so when he picked up and answered with his standard, "Cameron, Homicide,"

the last thing he expected to hear coming back at him was
the ruined bullfrog croak even twenty years worth of booze
and cigarettes hadn't changed all that much.

"Hello, son."

Cold shot through him. His scalp prickled. Something—an unrecognizable sound—came out of his mouth,
so he cleared his throat and tried again. This time managed
to produce a flat, "Dad."

His father's chuckle sounded more nervous than amused.
"I know, I'm the last person you probably expected to hear
from."

"That's about right," Alan drawled, and heard an
exhalation on the other end of the line.

"Yeah, well…Bucky called me, you know. Did you think
he wouldn't?" Alan didn't reply, and after a moment came
another exhalation. "I'm just sorry you didn't feel like you
could come to me, is all. Anyhow, I've got a name for you.
If you want it. Considering where it came from."

"Not a problem," Alan said. His heart was racing a mile
a minute and his jaws felt like they were wired together.
"If it'll help close this case, I'm sure as hell not going to
turn it down."

This time the chuckle sounded genuinely amused.
"Spoken like a cop, son. Guess the apple didn't fall all
that far from the tree. So—" he cleared his throat loudly
"—anyway, the guy's name is Faulkner—Bob Faulkner.
He was a homicide detective down in Baltimore—retired,
a'course—getting on in years, though. Met him a while
back—I forget now what the occasion was—and we got to
talking about old times, old cases. You know how it goes.
Anyways, he was telling us, Bucky and me, about this case
he had, way way back, but it stuck with him because, he
said, the kids were just so doggone nice, squeaky-clean, and

the case never did make any sense. Anyways, when Bucky told me you'd called, it was the first thing we thought of, both of us. Went ahead and looked him up—turns out he still lives in Bal'more. He's expecting your call, if you want to talk to him."

It was a moment or two before Alan could reply, and he had to clear his throat first. "Okay, I'll do that," he said. He listened to the number, jotted it down, then added, "Thanks."

"No problem. Glad I could help." There was a long silence, and then a gruff and raspy, "Think you could maybe give your old man a call sometime, when you're not so busy?"

The knot in Alan's chest became a fist, squeezing the breath out of him. "Sure. Yeah. I'll do that."

After he'd hung up, he sat for a few minutes, clammy and sweaty, waiting for his heart rate to slow down. When he looked up, he found Carl watching him.

His partner's somber expression brightened into a smile. "Hoo boy, for a minute there you looked like you were talking to a ghost."

Alan laughed without humor. "You could say that. That…was my dad."

"Seriously?" Alan nodded. Carl tilted his head thoughtfully. "Interesting…"

"Yeah," Alan said sourly. Glowering, he picked up the phone again, consulted the number he'd written down on a notepad and dialed it.

It was answered after four rings, by a voice that sounded out of breath. Alan was picturing a frail old geezer on oxygen, until, after he'd identified himself, he heard a robust cackle.

"Caught me a little ahead of myself," Bob Faulkner

said. "I was just lugging the file box up out of the damn basement. Gimme a minute...lemme catch my breath."

"Sure," Alan said, "take your time."

"Whoo—been a few years since I looked at those files. Used to haul 'em out every now and then, go through everything all over again...kept thinking I'd see something I'd missed. You know how it is. Or if you don't, you will. Every homicide cop, if he's on the job long enough, has one—the case that won't let him alone, you know? So... Lieutenant Cameron—that'd be your dad, I guess?"

"Right."

"Good man—good cop. He tells me you've got a case you think might be connected with this one?" The suppressed excitement in the old detective's voice came over the line, loud and clear.

"Maybe," Alan said cautiously. "Uh...you have any objections to my recording this call? Make it easier to go back over things."

"Sure, no problem."

Alan poked buttons, put the call on speaker, then said, "Okay, we're on. I'm looking for—" What could he say? A double homicide? But it hadn't been that, had it? "Might have been missing persons, *probable* homicide—young couple, maybe mid-twenties, early thirties at the most. Would have happened around the first of September, 1969."

"Time's right." Faulkner was silent for a moment. "So's the age. And it's interesting, you know, you calling it a 'probable' homicide. We had it as a missing persons case for a while, but I always did figure they was dead, leaving their kid behind like that."

Alan's scalp prickled. "They had a child?"

"Little boy. About five years old when they disappeared.

They'd left the kid with a neighbor and went out to dinner and a movie. It was the neighbor called the police when they didn't show up to collect the boy. Wasn't until the next day they found the couple's car in a downtown parking lot. Not a trace of the two of them, then or since." Faulkner made a tsking sound. "Shame. Nice kids. Really nice. That's what made it so hard, I think."

"What can you tell me about them?"

"James and Karen McKinney. Lord, sometimes I think I know those names better'n I know my own kids'. Squeaky-clean—I mean *really*. Not a thing in their past history, no debts, no vices, no enemies—hell, they hadn't been in town long enough to make enemies. They'd just moved here—came from someplace up in northern Pennsylvania, one of those dying coal-mining towns, you know? High school sweethearts—she was as pretty as a picture, and he was good-looking, too. They got married right outa high school and she got pregnant right off the bat, but they didn't let it hold 'em back. Nah, they were going places, those two. She went to work so he could go to college while her mother watched after the baby. Then her mom passed away about the time he graduated, and he got a job down here. Teaching—yeah, he was a damn schoolteacher, you believe that? Or woulda been. He was set to start the new job when school started, woulda been right after Labor Day, that's the way they did, back then. Way I always figured it, those two kids were out celebrating their last free weekend before the new job, the new school year started. And…poof. They just…disappeared off the face of the earth."

"People don't just disappear," Alan said. "You must have an idea, some kind of theory what might have happened."

There was another long pause. "Most everybody

thought it was probably a random thing—some psycho, you know?—and those kids just happened to be in the wrong place at the wrong time."

"*Most* everybody. But you don't think so."

"Didn't feel right to me—I don't know why. Well, for one thing, usually with those kinds of things, the bodies turn up sooner or later. Or else there's more killings. This was just too clean. Struck me as being…professional."

"Professional. As in…a *hit?*"

"I know, I know. The question is, *why?*" Another pause. "You wanna know what I think? If it *was* a hit, then somebody got it wrong, that's all."

"You mean—" Alan felt a sudden chill.

"Yeah. I think the reason those two kids got whacked, somebody made a mistake, got the wrong people. It was just a case of mistaken identity."

Alan didn't say anything. He couldn't. He felt queasy—physically sick.

"Yeah…I always did think it was kind of funny, because according to the landlord, the couple that had the apartment before the McKinneys moved in, seems they'd done a midnight flit—skedaddled in the middle of the night, left owing a month's rent. Woulda made sense, if they knew there was a contract out on them. Thing is, I looked into them, too. Nothing." After a moment Faulkner cleared his throat. "So, am I getting this right? Your dad says you think Karen McKinney might be alive? After all these years…"

There was a break in the old man's voice, and it struck Alan that Faulkner had spoken of the couple—the McKinneys—as if they were people he'd known personally and well. As maybe he had, he thought, maybe better than those who'd called themselves neighbors and friends of the couple, even family. He'd studied every detail of their personalities, their lives, had lived with them inside his head for years, even decades. They probably *were* as close to him as members of his own family.

"Too soon to tell," he said gently, not wanting to get the guy's hopes up in case the Jane Doe pulled out of the Chesapeake turned out to be unrelated to the Baltimore case. "Can you fax me whatever photos you have of Karen McKinney?"

"Sure can. I'll send you the whole damn file, soon as I get somebody to drive me to the post office. I don't drive in the city these days—too damn dangerous."

"Thanks," Alan said. "I do appreciate it."

"One more thing you should know."

"Yeah? What's that?"

"Remember I said it had been quite a few years since I'd looked at those files? Well, last time was...oh, maybe ten, fifteen years ago. Somebody else was looking into the case—came to see me in person, in fact."

"Really." Alan's spine had straightened involuntarily.

Faulkner chuckled. "That got your attention, didn't it? Yeah, fella was a private dick out of Atlanta. I've got his name right here, but I don't think he's in Atlanta anymore. I think he moved out west somewhere. But if he's still licensed, you ought to be able to locate him easily enough. P.I.'s name was Holt Kincaid. Said he was James and Karen McKinney's son."

Alan didn't have to look to know his partner had swiveled back to his computer and was already typing in the name. By the time he'd given Faulkner his fax number and the address where he could send the McKinney files, finished his goodbyes and signed off, Carl was sitting back, staring intently at his monitor screen.

"What've you got?"

Carl flicked him a glance. "Would you believe your P.I. lives in L.A. now? On Laurel Canyon. But that's not all."

Alan was on his feet, looking over the other man's shoulder. Carl tapped the screen. "Take a look. Could be a coincidence, I guess."

"You know what I think about coincidences," Alan muttered, then read aloud from the information on the screen. "Date of birth…November…1964." He shot Carl a look, but didn't point out the obvious. A moment later, he straightened up, one hand clamped to the top of his head. "Sonofa—" he whispered.

The full name given on the application form was James Holt Kincaid.

Jimmy?

Lindsey had been for a long run in Mission Bay Park that morning. She'd been doing a lot of running the whole past week, but today being Saturday, she'd decided to push herself. She was in the shower cooling off when she heard her doorbell ring, and because she wasn't expecting anyone, for a while she tried to ignore it. But obviously, whoever it was didn't seem inclined to give up. The ringing went on and on, sounding more and more insistent.

Finally, she swore, shut off the water, wrapped a towel around her head and shrugged into a short terry cloth robe. "Coming! I'm *coming,* already," she hollered, tying the robe's belt as she stomped angrily and barefooted down the stairs. In the entryway she took a quick look through the peephole. Then, as her insides performed what she knew to be physically impossible feats—her stomach dropped, her heart turned over, etc.—she looked again. And with shaking hands, unlocked and opened the door.

"Alan—uh, Detective Cameron," she managed to say, then stood clutching the collar of her robe and mopping self-consciously at her wet face with it, while her visitor pulled off his sunglasses and moved past her. He was dressed casually, in cargo pants and short-sleeved knit shirt with a collar, but in spite of that she could see he was in full cop mode, judging from the way he came into her house as if he had every right to be there.

"Right the first time," Alan said, with a brusque cheeriness she immediately recognized as false. His curious gaze swept over his surroundings, taking in the stairway, landing and high-vaulted ceiling. When she didn't respond immediately, he glanced at her and added dryly, "What I mean is, it's pretty silly for you to call me Detective Cameron, isn't it? After all, we've kissed."

"More than once...actually." Pleased with her own response—the offhanded coolness of it—she closed the front door, then unwound the towel from around her head and draped it over the banister. When she turned back to him, combing her damp hair back with her fingers, she saw that he was watching her, and that his smile was apologetic.

"Sorry," he said, as his eyes, no longer cop-bright, came to rest on her hair. "I did try to call first. You weren't answering your cell."

"I was running. I never take it with me when I run."

He nodded. "I remember that." There was an awkward pause.

She saw it then—the folder, standard manila-file type, clutched in his left hand, held down at his side. She gave a little gasp. "You've—did you find something?"

He lifted the folder and let it fall back to his side. "That's why I came. I have some things I want you to look at.

Seemed easier just to drive over. Sorry if I caught you at a bad time."

"No, no, that's all right. I...like I said, I'd been out for a run. I just got back, and was...well, as you can see." She laughed and gave him a sideways look. "I've been doing quite a bit of running this week, actually. Helps keep my mind off things...you know, like waiting for the phone to ring." She didn't tell him *he* was one of the things she'd been trying to keep off her mind. "Um, can I get you something to drink? I have diet soda, water...Or, I can make some coffee, if you'd rather."

"That sounds good. Sure. Coffee—if it's not too much trouble."

He seems edgy, she thought. *Almost...nervous. How unlike him...* Oddly, as if in response, her own heart began to beat faster.

"No trouble," she said as she led him past her tiny living room and into the roomy combination kitchen-dining area where she spent most of her time, since it doubled—or tripled—as her home-office space, as well. It was amazing how much smaller the space seemed with Alan Cameron in it. How crowded.

She measured beans and water into the coffeemaker and turned it on. She turned to find Alan gazing out the French doors that opened onto her patio, separated from the rest of the town house complex by a low stuccoed wall and tropical landscaping.

"The ocean is out there—you can't see it from down here, though. The real view is upstairs—" she pointed at the ceiling "—in my bedroom." She coughed nervously. "Um...we could sit outside, if you want to. That wind does seem to be getting colder, though. I think a storm might be coming in."

He nodded absently as he turned back to her. "It's moving down the coast. I think it's supposed to get here sometime tomorrow. That's okay—in here's fine." He placed the folder on the glass-topped table and pulled out a chair, then leaned on the back of it instead of sitting down. "I'm sorry I didn't get to this sooner. I've had a busy week. Spent a couple days testifying in court. That really takes a bite out of my time."

"No, no—that's perfectly...I understand. You have more important things to do, I'm sure."

"Actually...I don't. More urgently demanding of my time, maybe. Definitely not more important."

For some reason, she believed him—maybe because of the intent way he was looking at her. "What was it you wanted to show me?" She was beginning to feel quivery inside—nervous energy, she thought. Or maybe just plain old fear.

"You might want to sit down," he said gently.

She shook her head, once—sharp and quick. "No. I'm fine. Just...show me."

He nodded. Giving her one last, measuring look, he opened the folder and took out a photograph. Or rather, a copy of a photo, an 8x10 black-and-white portrait of a young woman, on plain white paper. He turned it and placed it on the tabletop.

She felt herself go icy cold...heard a roaring in her ears. The world seemed to shrink down to the size of that single photograph. She was vaguely aware of hearing a chair scrape across tile, then felt Alan's hands on her arms. Briefly—there and then gone.

"I told you you should sit down." His voice was harsh, but strangely, the more comforting because of that.

"I'd rather stand up." Somehow, she felt stronger on her

feet. Less vulnerable. She shook her head, frowning down at the photograph. "I'm okay now. It's just...kind of a shock. I mean—she's so young. It's my mother, isn't it?"

"I don't know," said Alan. He had his arms folded across his chest, now, and was regarding her narrowly. "Is it?"

She nodded, picked up the photo and held it...couldn't take her eyes off it. She touched the black-and-white image with her fingertips, as if she could actually feel the warmth of flesh-and-blood cheeks, the smoothness of the sleek pageboy hairdo. "The earliest picture I have of her is her wedding photo—when she married my dad." Her voice caught on the last word. She raised her eyes to Alan's. "When was this taken? Do you know? She looks so much younger...her face is fuller. She looks so happy."

"It's her senior picture. The one that would have been in her high school yearbook the year she graduated."

"But..." She stared at him. "I don't—does this mean you've found where she lived? Before the fire? Where she went to school?"

Alan took a deep breath. "Maybe. I think so." He held up a hand. "Look, I know you have a million questions. I don't have all the answers, not yet. I'll tell you everything I've found out so far, but first...I want you to look at one more photo for me, okay?"

She gripped the back of the chair he'd suggested she sit down in, wondering whether her knees would continue to hold her. And whether he would touch her again. She caught a quick sip of air and nodded.

Alan took a second sheet of paper out of the file and placed it on the table in front of her. This was another plain paper copy of an 8x10 black-and-white photo, although this one didn't have the too-polished look of the professional portrait. A young couple—they seemed impossibly young,

still just kids, really—stood before a table, in the process
of cutting a wedding cake. The table was covered with a
plain white cloth. The cake looked homemade. Both the
tablecloth and the cake were adorned with flowers of some
kind—possibly peonies, Lindsey thought. The bride wore
a simple white dress, sleeveless with a sweetheart neckline
and the tight-fitting bodice and full skirt that were the
style in the 1960s. Her dark hair was upswept, probably
in an effort to look more grown-up, and held in place with
a crown of flowers. The groom's hair was dark, too, cut
flat on top and slicked back on the sides, and his dark suit
looked a little too big for him. His hand covered his bride's
as she held the knife poised to make the first cut, and the
two gazed into each other's eyes and smiled.

"It's my mother, isn't it?" She asked the question before
she lifted her eyes to Alan's. She realized she was crying
when she saw him through a blur of tears.

"I don't know," he said again, cautiously. "Is it?"

"I think so." She touched her streaming nose with the
back of her hand, then whispered, shaking her head, "But
I don't know who *he* is. That's not my dad."

"Lindsey…"

"Who is that—that *boy?* That *man?*" She held up both
hands, backing away from him as he reached toward her.
"That's not my father! *That's not my dad!*"

Her hands were flat against his chest, her eyes squeezed
shut. Then his arms came around her, holding her tightly,
and now, instead of her hand it was her cheek that lay
against his chest. She drew a convulsive breath, and his
hand came to cradle her head, turning it so the sob that
burst from her was muffled in the warm crispness of his
shirt. He held her like that and let her cry, not saying

anything, only rearranging his arms to enfold her more closely and pressing his face against her damp hair.

And presently, when she'd grown quieter, he began to stroke her back, softly...gently...and she thought it was the most incredibly *good* thing she'd felt in a very long time. She couldn't remember any man ever touching her quite like that before, and it seemed the most natural thing in the world to lift her head from his shoulder and tilt her face up to his. And the most natural thing in the world for him to close the very small distance that remained, and kiss her.

Chapter 9

I am not sure what made me choose the woman to die first. I think perhaps I wanted to spare her the agony of watching her husband die. Maybe she had softened my heart, a little bit, after all. Yes, even then.

Excerpt from the confession of Alexi K.
FBI Files, Restricted Access,
Declassified 2010

For the first time, he kissed her without pretense or role-playing, with no one watching, no one to impress or mislead. Kissed her simply because he wanted to, and because it seemed so natural and right that it was almost impossible *not* to. Kissed her the way he wanted to, without counting the seconds—*Long enough? Too long?*—or worrying how an onlooker would judge it. *Too intimate? Not intimate enough?*

She smelled sweet, like shampoo and soap, but tasted of the salt tears she'd shed. Her lips quivered slightly when they first touched his. Then they grew soft, and warm…and became his, became a part of him, that part he kept locked away most of the time, the part that was gentle and giving and that needed, most of all, to love. It had been a long time since he'd opened up that part of himself to a woman, and he did so now with a sense of profound happiness. A ball of warmth filled his chest—warmth that felt like sunshine. Like joy.

Needing, finally, to release some of that happiness, he broke the kiss with a soft, bemused laugh, his hands cupping the rounds of her shoulders, gently kneading. She turned her face to one side and laughed, too, although the sound she made seemed more wounded than joyful. He wondered if it was that or his own need that prompted him to slide his hands upward along her neck to cradle her head when he should have been letting her go…saying no…stepping away. But then she tipped back her head and those thick lashes lifted, and he found himself gazing into those incredible eyes, and he didn't wonder or question or think a single moment longer.

For a long, long moment she looked into his eyes, while his thumbs stroked her temples, cheekbones…and into her hair. He watched her eyes grow slumberous, the lashes flutter down, and he dipped his head and, with great tenderness, kissed the dampness there. He brushed his lips across the velvety skin of her cheek and felt desire crawl along his nerve endings like flames licking oil. And when she let her head fall back into his hands, offering her throat to his questing mouth, he took it, but quivering with restraint, half-afraid of his own hunger.

Her breath escaped in a sigh, stirring his hair. He felt her move, shift slightly as she untied the belt on her robe, and he let his hands slide down, slipping under the robe, into the humid warmth beneath. She was so warm…her skin still moist and fragrant from her shower. Her bones, woman's bones, small and slight beneath silken skin and delicate muscle, nevertheless seemed to pulsate beneath his palms with strength and energy and life.

Desire flooded through him, all but overwhelmed him. He'd never known such hunger for a woman. Which is why it was such a shock to him when he heard his own voice saying, "No."

She murmured something, and he felt her sway under his hands, just a little, as if she'd been buffeted by an unexpected gust of wind. Feeling battered himself, he tugged her robe back together and stood for a moment with his eyes closed, breathing hard. "Bad idea," he murmured, half to himself. *On so many levels.*

She didn't argue with him. Didn't protest, or beg, or ask why, although he could feel her body trembling and knew she must be as overcome with desire and disappointment as he was.

"I'm sorry," he said in a rasping voice, and she only nodded, standing very still, neither moving toward him nor away.

It hit him, then, what a rare woman she was, and how much he *liked* her. Respected her. Valued her. *Wanted her.* Voices clamoured in the back of his mind—maybe in front of it, too—strident, derisive, frustrated, confounded voices. *You idiot, what more do you want? She suits you, in so many ways. She's everything you could ever want in a woman, and then some. She's perfect for you, and you're a fool. You're going to regret this.*

Probably. Almost certainly. Which only made it all the harder to tell himself this was the way it had to be.

Lindsey turned away from him, finally, one arm folded across her waist, hand clutching the collar of her robe. With the other she reached out and touched the photo of the wedding couple as she stared down at it.

"So," she said in a flat, muffled voice, "it's true then? My father is not my father, and my mother is not who I thought she was...it's all true?"

Alan had to clear his throat before he could answer her. "I'm still connecting the dots. I'll tell you everything I know so far, but if you don't mind, I'd like to do it on the way."

"On the way?" She lifted her head to frown at him. "Where?"

"That's...why I came over, actually. Do you have any plans for the rest of the day? This evening? We probably won't get back until pretty late."

"No—no, I don't have any plans... Back from where?"

"Los Angeles. One of those dots that needs connecting. A private investigator..." He caught a breath. No way in hell he was telling her who he suspected this private investigator might be, not when she was so vulnerable. Not when he was so susceptible to her vulnerability. He'd managed to tell himself no once; he wasn't sure he trusted himself to do it twice. "I think he might have some answers for us. He lives in Laurel Canyon, and according to his wife, he should be home and available to see us this evening. If we leave now, we can make it before dinnertime—it's a weekend, so traffic shouldn't be a problem." Although, he reminded himself, with the L.A. freeways, you never knew.

"Give me fifteen minutes," she said, and headed for the stairs.

He'd been right about the traffic, although he'd forgotten to take into account the storm traveling down the coast from its birthplace in the Gulf of Alaska. California's winter storms were late arriving this year; normally, by mid-November there would have been at least one good rain, but this year the jetstream had stayed stubbornly to the north, carrying the long-awaited rains off to the east before they had a chance to do more than sprinkle on Orange County and points south. It looked like this one might make it all the way to San Diego, good news for a city operating on permanent water conservation protocols.

Driving north on I-5 was like heading into night. With the short autumn day and the ominous darkening blue-gray sky ahead, most cars had their headlights on even though it was still mid-afternoon. As he drove, Alan told Lindsey what he and Carl had found out so far, being careful to lay out for her only the facts, keeping their suppositions to himself.

She sat quietly listening, looking through the contents of the file folder he'd brought, and when he'd finished, she tapped the printed copy of the article from the Richmond paper.

"And…you believe this woman, the one the fishermen found, is the same one that disappeared in Baltimore along with her husband? The one you believe is my mother?"

You ID'd her yourself, he thought, but only said cautiously, "It's a possibility. The timing's right."

She made an impatient gesture and dropped the article

back into her lap. "It's a terrible picture. I can't tell anything from this. Nobody can."

"She fits the general description," Alan pointed out. "And the head injury matches." He waited a beat, then added gently, "According to Richmond PD, a man claiming to be the woman's husband showed up three days later. Apparently, she had no memory of him whatsoever. He produced documents—a birth certificate and marriage license—as proof Jane Doe was his wife. According to those documents, the couple's names were Roger and Sally Phillips. She was released into his custody, and that was the last anyone saw or heard of them."

"Okay, so…?"

"Documents are easily forged. Don't forget, that was before computers and national and international databanks. Long before DNA. Wanna know what I think?" He gave her a quick glance and saw anger—or maybe tears—bright in her eyes. "I think Roger and Sally Phillips ceased to exist the day they walked out of that hospital in Richmond, Virginia. And that they were reborn sometime thereafter in San Diego, California, as Richard and Susan Merrill. And, there's one other thing." He paused, fortifying himself, knowing how hard this next bit of news was going to be for her. "When is your birthday?"

He heard her soft intake of air. "My birthday? May twelfth, 1970—why?"

Keeping his eyes fixed on the road ahead and his voice even, he told her. "According to the hospital records, Jane Doe, aka Sally Phillips, was approximately four weeks pregnant when she was fished out of the Chesapeake Bay in early September, 1969. She might not have even known herself she was pregnant, at the time. But her baby would have been born, most likely, sometime around the first to the middle of May…1970."

The silence inside the car seemed profound, even eclipsing the roar of freeway traffic beyond the windows.

Alan said, "Lin—" but got no further before she interrupted, shaking her head vehemently

"Don't. Just…don't…say anything."

He waited patiently while she struggled with it, and wasn't surprised when she finally drew a reinforcing breath and spoke in a calm voice, tight with self-control. "I don't care what you think. I *will not* believe my father—my *dad*—could have done anything to hurt, much less *kill*, my mother. Maybe he did claim her at the hospital, even gave a fake name—and you don't have any proof he did, by the way, do you?" Alan shook his head. She settled back in her seat. "Even if he did, that doesn't mean he was the one who shot her."

"She says he is," Alan reminded her.

She dismissed that with a gesture. "She's confused. Why on *earth* would he try to kill her, then—" her voice wobbled and she caught a breath in an unsuccessful attempt to control it "—take her home and…care for her all those years? Why would someone do that? He *loved* her. He loved *me.* It doesn't make any sense."

The tears in her voice were hard to listen to. He felt them like a weight on his shoulders, and shifted irritably, trying to ease the burden. "Dammit, Lindsey, I know it may not make sense to you. But the facts—"

"Facts? You don't have facts, you have theories!"

"Theories that fit the facts. Face it—your father, the man you know as Richard Merrill, has been lying to you all your life. He's not who you believed him to be. When are you going to accept that, and deal with the truth?"

She turned to him in a fury. "And when are you going to understand? This is my *father*. The man who was always there for me. How would *you* feel if it were *your* father? Your dad who—"

"My *father*," Alan lashed back, "was an abusive jerk who drove my mother to drink and eventually to suicide. He was never there for either one of us, and quite frankly, it's been a long time since I felt anything for him whatsoever."

Silence once again enveloped the car. For several minutes the only sounds he was aware of were the thumping of his own heartbeat and the voice inside his head reading him the riot act for unloading on Lindsey like that. He wished he could say he didn't know where his outburst had come from, but of course he did know. Hearing his old man's voice after so many years had definitely stirred up some sleeping demons. But she sure didn't deserve the fallout.

He was searching for a way to apologize to her when she drew a quick, unsteady breath and said, "Well. I guess that explains a lot."

Yeah, he supposed it did. He gave a humorless snort of laughter and didn't say anything, but he was thinking it was a damn good thing he'd told himself no, earlier, when he'd been on the brink of making a huge mistake. There was just no way in hell it was ever going to work between him and Lindsey Merrill, no matter how much he liked, respected, admired and wanted her.

And God help me, I do want her. Still.

They made good time. Traffic was open and fairly free-flowing all the way into downtown L.A. Since it was still early enough, they didn't have to contend with Music Center traffic. There was some congestion around the I-5/101 interchange, which Lindsey imagined was pretty standard, even early on a Saturday evening, but at least it wasn't raining. The Alaskan Express seemed to be holding off, for the moment.

When they exited the freeway onto Hollywood Boulevard, she was startled to see the streets already festooned with holiday decorations beginning to sway, now, in the winds that heralded the storm's imminent arrival. Christmas had seemed a long way off in San Diego—or maybe she'd just been too preoccupied with her own troubles to notice.

The first raindrops smacked onto the windshield as they turned onto Laurel Canyon Boulevard where, thankfully, most of the traffic seemed to be going the other way, as residents of the Valley headed for the entertainment centers in Hollywood and Los Angeles. Even armed with a Mapquest printout and with Lindsey helping to search for house numbers, they drove past the address the first time and had to go up to Mulholland Drive to turn around. But at last they pulled into the miniscule driveway in front of a street-level garage tucked up against the steep side of the canyon.

Alan turned off the motor, and for a few minutes they sat, not talking, listening to the ticking of the cooling engine, the patter of rain on the roof of the car, and the swish of cars passing by on the street behind them, neither of them, apparently, quite ready to face what lay ahead. Lindsey watched Alan's fingers tapping restlessly on the steering wheel, then looked over at him. Silhouetted intermittently against the headlights, his profile seemed tense…even grim.

"What's wrong?" she asked after a moment. *What aren't you telling me?*

He shook his head but didn't reply.

"Alan?" Unexpectedly, her voice had begun to tremble.

"Okay, you'd better tell me why we're here, because I'm not getting out of this car until you do. You told me this man is a private investigator who once looked into the case of that couple missing from Baltimore. You said he might have some details, be able to fill in some blanks."

"That's true."

"What else?"

He turned to look at her, finally, and his eyes seemed intent in the half-light. "Didn't you wonder *why* he was looking into the couple's disappearance? What his interest was?"

She shook her head, not understanding—quite— but beginning to. "I didn't—I guess it didn't—I just thought…"

He let out an exasperated breath. "Lindsey, this guy's name is James Holt Kincaid." He paused while she took that in, and when he went on, his voice was gentler. "He was looking into the disappearance because James and Karen McKinney were his *parents*." Another pause. "He was five years old when they went missing."

Lindsey stared at him. She didn't say anything because she couldn't. Couldn't speak, couldn't even seem to breathe. She felt cold—with shock, perhaps—then slowly began to shiver, but with anger, not cold. She swallowed once while he waited patiently, then again, fighting for control. After several moments she managed to say quietly, "You think this is 'Jimmy,' don't you?"

He wouldn't look at her. Staring at the windshield, he gave a cautious shrug. "It's a possibility. Or, it could be a coincidence. Jimmy's a pretty common name."

The initial shock of the bombshell was wearing off, and the full implications of what he'd told her were sinking in. "Which would make him my brother, if everything else you've told me is true." She paused...waited. Willing him to look at her. At last she said thickly, "When were you going to tell me?"

He didn't answer...still wouldn't look at her. Rage buffeted her, echoing the gusts of wind that now were slamming into the car. She lifted a hand and clenched it into a fist, wishing it was in her to actually hit him with it. Instead, she let it fall limp into her lap and drew a sobbing breath. "When, Alan? *Were* you going to tell me?"

He gave himself a little shake, and his voice, when it came, was gruff. "I wasn't sure. I wanted to get your impressions of the man, without any interference...from emotions. I'm sorry. I guess I just couldn't do it." He threw her a look she couldn't read in the dim light and yanked at the door handle. "One thing's for sure. We aren't going to find those answers sitting here. Let's go talk to Mr. Kincaid."

What could she do? Still shaken, still furious, battered by emotions she didn't know how to deal with—*I have a brother? Oh, my God, Can it be true? I have a brother!*— Lindsey opened her door and stepped out into the wind and spattering rain.

There was an iron gate to the right of the garage. When they approached it, a floodlight came on. Alan pressed a button beside an intercom box and spoke into it, giving their names. A moment later the gate slid open to admit them, then creaked shut behind them. As Lindsey followed Alan up zigzagging stone steps, above their heads the wind lashed trailing branches of eucalyptus trees so huge and old their tops were lost in the darkness and rain. The air was pungent with their scent.

When she looked up, trying to make out her surroundings through the rain, she saw that someone was waiting for them on the wooden deck at the top of the stairs. A man, bareheaded in the storm, wearing a long-sleeved dark pullover, hands tucked in the pockets of his jeans. Her legs weakened; she stumbled, and instantly Alan whipped around and his hand was there to steady her, then hold her elbow firmly as he brought her the last few steps remaining. The man on the deck opened the gate in the low wooden railing that surrounded it and held it for them, then closed it after them and thrust out his hand. Grasping Alan's in both of his, he spoke in a voice raised above the rushing sound of the storm.

"Detective Cameron? I'm Holt Kincaid."

"I'm Alan. And this is Lindsey."

Lindsey felt her hand swallowed up by a larger and warmer one; other than that, she was numb.

Holt Kincaid seemed oblivious to the rain that spangled his hair and shoulders and was beginning to drip from the end of his nose. He paused for a moment to look searchingly into her face, then abruptly gestured, urging them to follow him.

"Come inside—this rain's great, isn't it?"

"We needed it," Alan agreed.

He held the door and they stepped into a sunroom, cozy with woven sisal floor mats and wicker furniture with thick, flowered cushions. A playpen occupied one corner of the room, and an assortment of toys were scattered here and there on the cushions and floor. Pots filled with green and flowering plants were everywhere, sitting on the floor and tabletops and hanging from ceiling beams, and Lindsey was reminded suddenly, painfully, of her mother. Thinking how she would love this room….

Their host led them on through a small kitchen that was separated by a wide countertop eating area from a den-like living room. The living room walls were covered in unstylish driftwood paneling, and a gas log burned in a fieldstone fireplace, turned down low. Because she still felt chilled, Lindsey went to stand in front of the fireplace, rubbing her hands together as she held them toward the warmth.

"Please—make yourselves comfortable," Holt said. "My wife will be right out—she's putting the baby down."

"You have a child?" It was Alan who asked the question as if he hadn't noticed the evidence, which she thought was unlikely. Lindsey turned just in time to catch the smile that burst over Holt's angular face.

Her breath caught. *My God. It's my mother's smile.*

"We do," Holt said, beaming and obviously besotted. "Our son Jamie's just fourteen months old. Now that he's walking, we're actively looking for a bigger place—one with a yard he can actually run around in. This has been great for the two of us, but—" he spread his arms to encompass not only the room but the whole outdoors "—as you can see, it's not exactly kid-friendly."

"Interesting, though," Alan commented.

"Uh…can I get you something to drink?" Holt clasped his hands together in a way that betrayed his own nervousness—and for some reason, lessened Lindsey's. "Are you hungry?"

He looked straight at her, then, and she realized she'd been blatantly staring at him. Now she saw his eyes clearly for the first time. They were her eyes.

Her stomach felt hollow, but she was too queasy to eat. She shook her head. Holt said, "Coffee, then?"

"Yeah," Alan said, "coffee would be great. Thanks."

As he busied himself in the kitchen, assembling coffee and accoutrements with the efficiency that suggested a long period of bachelorhood in his past, Holt spoke to them across the counter, picking up Alan's previous comment.

"Yeah," he said, "this canyon does have its history."

"More like legends," Alan said. "Wasn't this a hippie mecca during the sixties and seventies? I've heard it was a big-time music scene—rock 'n roll, not to mention sex and drugs."

Holt chuckled. "Oh, yeah. Even before that, though, the Canyon seems to have attracted characters—a lot of them famous. Or infamous. Still does, although it's more gentrified nowadays. But—" he dusted his hands, having completed his task, and aimed a piercing look across the room to where Lindsey still stood with her back to the fire "—you didn't come for a Laurel Canyon history seminar."

He came around the counter, carrying a tray laden with four cups of steaming coffee, spoons and crockery containers of cream, sugar and sweetener. He placed the tray on the coffee table in front of Alan, then picked up the folder that was lying there.

"This it?"

Alan nodded. "That's it."

Holt opened the folder. Standing, he went through its contents one page at a time, studying each one before carefully turning it facedown on the left side of the folder. When he'd finished, he sank heavily into a chair across from Alan, the folder still open across his knees. He shook his head. "How could I have missed this? How did Baltimore PD miss this?"

Alan helped himself to a cup of coffee and took a sip of it—black—before he answered. "There wasn't any reason for it to show up on Baltimore's radar—or yours, either. She didn't stay a Jane Doe long enough. Her husband showed up, ID'd her. Nobody questioned it."

Holt sat for a long moment in silence, staring down at the folder. Then he looked up at Lindsey, and his eyes were gentle. Compassionate. "This must be a tough time for you."

She managed to smile, even laugh, a little. "Oh, yeah."

He held up the photo of the young Karen McKinney. "This is my mother. I understand you…think it might be your mother, too."

She nodded, fighting back tears. Holt said, without smiling, "Well, then, obviously, that would make you my sister." She nodded again, hugging herself tightly; it was all she could do, it seemed, without breaking down. Holt shook his head and simply said, "Wow."

Lindsey thought, *He's as shaken by this as I am.*

And as before, the awareness brought her a measure of calm. She said softly, "This must be hard for you, too. Finding out your mother is alive, after all these years."

"*Might* be alive," Alan broke in, his voice harsh. "We're still lacking absolute proof."

"Which, thank God, we can get easily enough," Holt said briskly. "I'll make sure you get a DNA sample before you leave." He closed the folder but held on to it. "But seems to me we have a pretty strong connection here…."

"Connect the dots…" Lindsey murmured, but nobody paid any attention to her.

So, she stood silently and watched them, the two men who had come into her life so unexpectedly and with such catastrophic effect. It struck her how alike they were, without actually *looking* alike. Same approximate age, similar coloring—dark hair and blue eyes—although

Holt had more silver in his hair and deeper creases around his eyes and mouth, and his eyes weren't quite as hard and steely as Alan's. They were of similar build and body type, too—tall but not extraordinarily so, slim but muscular—although Alan was more powerfully built. A memory—the glimpse she'd had of him naked to the waist, mopping water drops from his neck and chest—flashed into her mind, and something inside her chest did a peculiar dropping-squeezing maneuver that made her catch her breath, inaudibly, guiltily...

"I agree," Alan said, setting his coffee down and leaning toward the other man, elbows on his knees. He counted, raising and touching one finger at a time, and Lindsey found herself riveted by the graceful economy of his movements. "One, the McKinneys are abducted from a movie theater parking lot in Baltimore. Two, two days later a Jane Doe matching Karen McKinney's description is pulled out of the Chesapeake, sporting a head wound that appears to have been caused by a bullet crease. Three, three days after that she's identified by a man claiming to be her husband, as Sally Phillips, his wife, who is also discovered to be in the early weeks of pregnancy."

He paused then, as a young woman came into the room, moving quietly to stand behind her husband's chair. She was small and slender, with short blond hair cut in shaggy layers. Dressed in jeans and a T-shirt, she seemed very young, barely more than a girl—until she leaned forward into the light, and Lindsey saw that her face wore the kind of serenity that only comes from having lived through the worst life has to offer, and emerged whole and happy on the other side.

Holt looked up, smiled, and took the hand she'd placed

on his shoulder. "Hey, there you are. Alan, Lindsey—like to have you meet my wife, Brenna."

Alan, who had risen with old-fashioned courtesy, nodded and said, "Nice meeting you, Brenna."

Lindsey nodded, too, and murmured, "Hi."

"Don't let me interrupt," Brenna said. Her voice had a raspy, husky quality, and her eyes were a shade of golden hazel that seemed only a shade or two darker than her hair.

Alan smiled at her and continued. "And…four, Richard and Susan Merrill appear in San Diego, California, Susan gives birth to Lindsey roughly eight months later. Oh—and Susan Merrill also happens to have a scar on her head that closely corresponds to Sally Phillips's head wound. And, has no record or memory of a past prior to San Diego."

"Seems like a no-brainer to me," Brenna said with a shrug.

Holt nodded, but then let out a breath in a frustrated gust. "Okay, I'm pretty much convinced. It all makes sense, except for one thing—*why?*"

Chapter 10

But when the man threw himself in front of her and my bullet went wild and missed its mark, I knew I had made a terrible—perhaps fatal—mistake.

He fought like a demon, even though his hands were bound. It was several minutes before I could regain control of the situation, and by that time, the woman had vanished in the darkness and fog. I searched, but could find no trace of her. At that point I could only hope the ocean had taken her after all.

Excerpt from the confession of Alexi K.
FBI Files, Restricted Access,
Declassified 2010

No one spoke. Holt looked at Alan, then Lindsey. After a long moment, he repeated it, in a voice rigidly controlled. "Why were they taken? There was no reason for them to be targeted—none whatsoever. That's what's always confounded me. It's what confounded Baltimore PD. It's damn hard to solve a case," he growled, "when there's absolutely no motive. No suspects. Nothing that makes any kind of sense."

Alan cleared his throat. "Well, there is one thing."

So Alan told him what Bob Faulkner, the retired Baltimore homicide cop, had said.

When he'd finished, Holt was staring at him, stony-faced. Brenna sat down on the arm of his chair and put her arm across her husband's shoulders.

Lindsey whispered, "A *mistake?*" Her face was pale with shock. Alan wanted to go to her, tell her to sit down, for God's sake. Hold her. But of course he didn't.

They all sat in silence, listening to the noise the rain and wind made as if fascinated by it—such unfamiliar sounds in that part of the world. Alan thought there probably weren't any words that could have expressed what they must be feeling, these two people whose lives had been turned upside down—forty years apart in time—by someone's *mistake.*

If that's what it had been.

Brenna rose abruptly. "Anybody want more coffee?"

"Yeah, Billie—thanks," Holt said absently, and Alan said, *"Billie?"* He was tuned to pet names, it seemed.

Brenna turned to smile at her husband, but only said, "Long story."

While they waited for the coffee, Holt made a visible effort to pull himself together and asked Lindsey to tell him about her mother.

His mother, too, Alan reminded himself. Most likely. There was real poignancy in that, he thought, but he had fortified himself against it; wallowing in the tragedy of these people's lives, he told himself, wasn't going to help solve the mystery of what had happened to Karen and James McKinney, and why.

He listened to Lindsey talk with only half of his attention, while he watched her avidly—watched the two of them, of course, but mostly Lindsey. It struck him how alike they were—not surprising, considering they were almost certainly brother and sister. He didn't need DNA to know that, it was right there in front of him. They had the same general body type—tall and slim, athletic build. And the same thick dark hair—although Holt's was a little more wavy and beginning to gray at the temples—and those same thick-lashed blue eyes.

Although Holt's didn't have quite the same effect on him Lindsey's had.

What was it, he wondered, that made one particular person's face so arresting to another? That made one face stick in his mind? Made him want to go on looking at it, never tire of watching it? He had no answers.

At one point he happened to glance over at Brenna, and found her watching *him*—watching him watch Lindsey—and there was something in her eyes...in her smile...that said, *Yes, I know. I understand how you feel.*

The cold squeezing sensation he felt in his belly was *fear.*

I can't do this, he thought. *Fall in love with her? Can't happen. Can't let it happen. No way.*

"Look at the time," he said abruptly, sitting up and glancing pointedly at his watch. "Lindsey—long drive ahead of us. We've kept you people long enough—didn't realize it was getting so late." He was on his feet, and instantly so were Holt, Brenna and Lindsey. Lindsey looked red-eyed and exhausted.

"Tomorrow's Sunday," Holt reminded him. "We can sleep in—well, one of us can," he added ruefully when his wife gave a huff of laughter and poked him with her elbow. "I guess with a toddler in the house, there's no such thing as a lazy morning. But, hey, you two should think about getting a hotel room, staying in town overnight. Drive back tomorrow. You know the freeways are going to be a nightmare with the rain. Wish we had a place to put you, but—"

He and Lindsey both assured him they would be fine, as he'd said, tomorrow was Sunday, they had plenty of time. Eventually, they were able to take their leave, amid clasped hands and hugs and exchanges of addresses and phone numbers, including cell phones, and promises to keep each other up-to-date and in close touch. Alan had Holt's DNA on a swab in a sealed evidence bag safely tucked away in his pocket.

In spite of the rain and the lateness of the hour—nearly midnight—being Saturday night, Hollywood was still clogged with traffic. Alan turned west on Sunset, figuring to make his way to the 405 freeway and thus avoid the nightmare through downtown L.A. However, the San Diego Freeway was also moving at a crawl, which was no big surprise to Alan. He'd become familiar over the years with Southern California drivers' customary response to wet roads, which was to proceed at normal speed in complete disregard of the fact that a little moisture on top of several months' buildup of oily scum would turn roadways into skating rinks.

After crawling along for half an hour or so, he looked at Lindsey and said, "What do you think?"

She looked back at him and said, "It's up to you, you're the driver."

So, he took the next exit and headed toward Santa Monica. Not being familiar with that town, he headed straight for the beach, figuring that would be the most likely place to find hotels with vacancies on a rainy November night. He chose the first big franchise hotel he saw—a Holiday Inn, right on the beach—and left Lindsey in the car while he went in to ask about vacancies. He was lucky; two adjoining rooms were available on the fifth floor on the side of the hotel that overlooked the ocean. He put the rooms on his personal credit card, then went back outside to the car. The rain was still coming down hard, a rush of sound that muffled but didn't drown the occasional boom of a wave thumping down on the shore at high tide. He slipped behind the wheel and slammed the door, cutting off the noise of storm and sea.

"Got us a couple of rooms," he said, and Lindsey nodded.

The silence seemed to wait for something more, and Alan knew there were things that probably needed to be said but didn't know what they were or how to say them. So, after a moment he started up the car and drove into the parking garage. As they waited for the elevator, he asked her if she was hungry. She shook her head. The elevator arrived and they rode up to the fifth floor in silence.

"Guess it's this way," he said, and took her elbow to steer her to the right as they got off the elevator. They walked side by side down the silent hallway, not looking at each other, looking at the numbers on the doors they passed.

"Here we are," he said, stopping at the first of the two rooms. He fished the plastic room keys out of his pocket, selected one. "You take this one—I'll be in the next one down." He unlocked the door, pushed it open, stepped inside. A light had been left burning over the desk. He looked around, out of habit, mostly. Satisfied the place was secure, he handed Lindsey her key. "Looks okay. Well... have a good night—see you in the morning."

He paused, and she nodded. He turned and headed for the door, knowing he should ask her if she needed anything. If she was going to be okay. He didn't, probably because he was afraid of what her answer would be. And because he didn't trust his own response.

Coward. The voice inside his head was so strident, for a moment he actually hesitated, wondering if it could have been spoken out loud, not just in his own mind. He glanced back at her, but she was standing exactly as he'd left her, pupils so dilated in the dim light that her eyes looked like black holes in a white mask. He went out and shut the door firmly behind him.

In his own room, he repeated the automatic check, then crossed to the closed curtains and opened them onto the vast darkness outside. He took off his jacket and draped it on the back of the chair in front of the desk, reached for his holster before he remembered he wasn't wearing it. He emptied his pockets onto the desktop—wallet, car keys, evidence bag with Kincaid's DNA sample, some small change and the hotel key. He pulled his shirt off and was heading for the bathroom when the knock came.

His heart jolted, but not as hard as it should have, and he realized he'd been waiting for the knock. Expecting it. *Hoping for it?*

Tossing his shirt onto the bed, he strode to the door, glanced briefly through the peephole, then opened it. "Lindsey?" he said.

She didn't look the way he'd expected her to—although what that was, he couldn't have said. She looked...angry, he thought.

"I *hurt*," she said. Her steady gaze seemed accusing.

"I know," he said gently.

"No—you don't. I don't think you do. I mean, it really hurts—here, and here, and here. Physically." She touched her face, her throat, her chest. "It hurts so bad, I wish I could take aspirin or something for it, but I know it wouldn't help." She took a breath, a shallow one, as if even that hurt. He stood back and made way for her to come in, but she stayed where she was, glaring at him. "I can't stop thinking about them."

"Who?" he asked, although he knew.

"*Them*—all of them. My mother, my father, those two people in the wedding picture, Holt, Jimmy, my dad. I keep seeing their faces…they're in my head. And every time I see them, I hurt."

"Empathy sucks," he said, nodding.

"I can't seem to stop it. I just…want…to make it…*stop*."

"That's a dangerous frame of mind to be in."

She nodded, and a frown made lines between her brows. "I know. I guess that's why people drink. Or take drugs. Or kill themselves."

"That's why my mother did." He hadn't known he was going to say that.

Her gaze didn't waver, and he wasn't sure she'd heard him. He decided he hoped she hadn't. "I wouldn't. But I thought of something else, and it seems to help."

"What's that?"

She snatched another breath, as if they were suddenly in critically short supply. "I thought of you. And the pain got a lot better. So, I thought I'd find out if seeing you in person would help even more."

"And does it?" he asked somberly, a quiver of tender laughter deep within his chest.

"Yes." Finally, she walked past him and into the room. He closed the door, then turned to find her gazing at him, arms wrapped across her body, eyes fierce and bright. "I keep thinking about how it felt when you held me the other day. I've thought about it quite a lot, actually. I thought it felt very, very good."

"Yes," Alan said. "I thought so, too."

"So," she said on another breath, "maybe you wouldn't mind too much, holding me right now." She gave him only a split second, then rushed on. "I know you think it's a bad idea—I get that. I just want you to know I won't expect anything—"

"Hush," he said, and folded her into his arms.

But, after a small, faint gasp, she went on talking. "Except tonight. I just need you to get me through this night. Please help me…"

"Like the song says?" he asked with a husky laugh.

She pulled back to stare at him. "What song?"

"'Help Me Make It Through The Night…'"

Nestled once more against his chest, her laugh was a tiny whimper of sound. "Oh. I was thinking of, 'Make The World Go Away.'"

"I guess this probably beats the hell out of a bottle of Scotch," he said after a moment, when neither of them had moved.

"I've never been much of a drinker," she whispered, turning her face toward his.

"Me, neither."

What the hell, he thought as he took her mouth. It wasn't the first time he'd known something was a bad idea and gone ahead and done it anyway.

* * *

She was glad when he turned the light off. Less glad that he didn't undress her. Leaving that choice up to her might have derailed the whole thing, if she'd been less determined. Less desperate. But she'd disengaged her thinking mind when she'd left her room and gone to knock on his door, and it was without thinking that she took off her clothes in the kindly darkness and laid them neatly over the room's only upholstered chair. She turned back toward him, and watched him in the faint light that leaked into the room from outside the uncurtained window, watched him tug the bedcovers back, then hold out his hand to her. She took it, and he drew her to the bed, then got in and held the covers open for her. Once again, leaving the choice up to her. She could come to him…or not.

She felt her heart thumping with appalling force inside her chest. Moving in a dream, not thinking, she sat on the edge of the mattress and lay down beside him. The cool, crisp sheets settled over them both.

She lay in the darkness with the rain pulling a curtain of sound around them, shivering at first, curled tightly against him—this man she barely knew—with her fist nested in his chest hair, the thump-thump of his heart loud in her ear and her hand rising and falling with his slow, even breaths. She closed her eyes, and the images came and played through her mind like an old-time newsreel, the faces, one after the other: A lovely young girl, the bride and her groom… like children playing at a make-believe wedding. A little boy, laughing and fat in his snowsuit, throwing snow at his mother. Her mother and father—her daddy, the one she knew and adored—gazing at her with love and pride. Her mother's face as she'd seen it last, haunted and terrified… her dad's face growing sadder and sadder by the day. Holt

Kincaid, a grown man asking in a man's voice a child's question: *Why?*

The pain came and this time she didn't fight it but let it wash over her in waves and waves, and he—this hardened cop, this man she barely knew—stroked her gently, so gently, until gradually the pain subsided and the shivering stopped and her body grew heavy and supple, and unfurled along his side the way a flower opens in the sun.

"I should have known you'd be so gentle," she whispered. "So kind. You are a kind, gentle man, Detective Cameron."

He gave a snort of laughter and growled, "That's just what every homicide cop wants to hear."

"I'm sorry. It's true, though."

"How do you know? You don't know me that well."

"Maybe not well, but I know *that*. I saw it that first day I met you, you know—the way you were with my mother."

He didn't reply, and after a moment she added, "I knew that you wouldn't turn me away, even if you do think you shouldn't—"

"Hush," he said for the second time, and raised himself so that he loomed above her, big and solid in the darkness. His head swooped down, blotting out what light there was, and his mouth found hers unerringly.

She gave a gasp and sank into it—the sheer pleasure of being kissed, held, stroked. Sank into it as she would a hot tub, sighing with the pure sensual pleasure.

After a while—she lost all track of time—he lifted his head and said in a soft growl, "Maybe I'm not all that kind. Maybe I just want to make love to you. Did you ever think of that?"

She laughed, and just as softly growled back, "That's okay, too. Make love to me, then."

Her eyes closed and she didn't notice or care; her body was doing what it wanted, with no direction from her thinking mind. She felt his lips brush her eyelids... his hands cradle her head while his thumbs stroked her cheeks...so lightly, so tenderly.

And it was the tenderness that was her undoing.

Prickles washed through her body in a stinging shower, a wave of longing that caught her unawares. It was pain, yes, but different from the other, the pain that had weighed her down and brought her to this almost-stranger's bed in the dead of night. This was bright and breathtaking, and she let herself be carried on it, into a realm of fantasy...of possibility...of *what if?*

What if this wasn't just for tonight, but for always?

What if it wasn't just making *love, but* love?

What if I love him?

What if he could love me?

What if he does?

So easily, the lines between fantasy and reality blurred and ran, like watercolors in the rain. She felt as if she'd always known him, this man who held her and touched her so tenderly. His hands seemed to know her body better than she did. His mouth, his fingers, his body came into her most intimate places, not as explorers, but as loved ones welcomed home.

She felt safe in his hands. Beyond the gentleness, there was strength in this man. How did she know that? It wasn't something she asked herself, then, her mind having disengaged from her body. It was just something her body *knew.* She was safe in his hands.

"Make love to me," she whispered, not even remembering she'd already said it.

* * *

He didn't reply with words, but simply did as she asked.

He'd never known a woman like this, so completely immersed in the act of making love, so utterly without reservation, self-consciousness or inhibition. Yet, not in a frantic way. Her body was pliant…relaxed, her movements so languorous and sweet he felt as though he could sink into her and lose himself there completely.

Her joy, her pleasure, her delight in his touch, his kisses, made him feel bigger, better, stronger. *More.* More of everything good and admirable than he'd ever felt in his life before. He felt blessed and yet humbled, as if he'd been entrusted with a great treasure to cherish and protect. Which should have been daunting, perhaps, except he also felt completely up to the task. Not only that, it seemed to him he was the only man alive who would be.

She sighed when he kissed her…swelled under his hands. He no longer heard the rain or saw the darkness, because the world was her, and him…nothing more. Just the two of them and then, so easily, so naturally, one.

Being inside her seemed so *right,* the only place he could be, then, the only place he felt he belonged, as if he'd come home after a long, long time in exile. He felt a swelling in his chest, an unanticipated sting behind his eyelids, and quickly ducked his head to claim her mouth again, releasing emotions in a way he could understand and allow—in passion.

Reaching under her, he drew her more closely against him and seated himself even more deeply inside her, and felt her move with him as if she were truly part of him, not a separate person at all. He didn't ask himself, *How can this be? How is it possible I've never made love with this woman before?* Not then. It was only later that it occurred to him to wonder, and ask: Where was the strangeness, the getting-to-know-you awkwardness that went with having sex with someone for the first time?

But just then, at that moment, he could only go with it, immerse himself in it as she did.

They moved together in the same rhythms for an unmeasured time, letting their bodies set the pace, tuned to each other as if they listened to the same music. And when the music rose finally to its crescendo, they rode it out together, bodies arching, swelling, pulsing and clenching in tandem. They clung together, first in something akin to terror, then exhilaration, and finally, a kind of thankfulness…and sweet relief.

Afterward, they lay intertwined and uncovered, bodies slick and humid where they touched, already beginning to feel the chill where they didn't. Even so, when he took his arm away from her to reach for the covers, she gave a little growl of protest.

He laughed softly and kissed her forehead, and when he had them covered up, gathered her close again. He heard her sigh, and for a few minutes more, let himself drift in the kind of contentment he hadn't believed himself capable of. But as his body cooled, inevitably so did his mind. Reason returned. And responsibility.

Still holding Lindsey close to his side with one arm, he lay back on the pillows and swore, muttering under his breath.

From her nest on his shoulder the murmur came, "Regretting it already?"

He shook his head. "No, it's not that. Regretting my own stupidity, I guess. And no—" he raised up to touch a kiss to her forehead "—I didn't mean that, either. What I mean is, I didn't even think about protection. I'm sorry. I think I even have a couple of condoms over there in my wallet. I just…forgot."

"You can't get me pregnant," she said after a moment. "And I haven't had sex since my divorce. I think I would know if I was…you know."

"And I was tested fairly recently—got sliced up by a suspect in a domestic abuse case, so they tested me as a precaution. But that's—"

"Is that what this is?" Her fingers traced the newly healed scar on his side, making him wince involuntarily. "Oh—sorry," she cried. "Did I hurt you?"

"No, you didn't. But what I was going to say was, that's no excuse. I should have remembered." He let out a breath. "Well—"

He stopped, but the words he'd been about to say hung there between them, unspoken: *Next time…*

Would there be a next time? Tonight…maybe. Even probably—or today, since it was already Sunday. But beyond that? He couldn't see it.

Her voice came, quietly and without much expression. "You do regret it, don't you."

"How could I regret what was probably one of the most amazing experiences of my life?" He felt exasperated, cornered, unnerved by his own unprecedented honesty.

She was silent for a moment, absorbing what he'd said. Then she drew a shaken breath and said, "It was for me, too. But I'm betting you're not thinking the same things I am right now."

"For instance?" It was a growl of futile belligerence.

"You don't want this—what just happened between us—to happen again."

"Not true." Again…futile. His body was already calling him a liar, and she knew it.

"I don't mean tonight," she said, with both a smile and sadness in her voice. "You said once, this—us—is a bad idea. You still think so."

"It's not a matter of what I think, or want," he said slowly, as if speaking to someone of limited intelligence. "It's just what *is*."

"Why? Is it because I'm part of a case you're working on?"

"Partly."

"What, is it against the law for a police officer to be involved with someone connected with an open case? Even if she's not a suspect?"

He stirred restlessly, his thoughts becoming scrambled… scattered. Fatigue, he wondered, or the distraction of her body lying warm and round against him. "No, not against the law."

"Department policy, then?" She stirred, too, and he felt her hand move, innocent of design, across his belly.

His voice seemed to come from there—deep in his belly. "Yeah, probably. Ethically…"

"So—it's *your* policy. Your ethics."

His laugh was harsh. "God, that makes me sound like such a prick."

Her hand grew still. "I don't mean for it to. I'm trying to understand. You're a man of principle—I understand that. It's one of the things that makes me…" She didn't finish it, and instead, after a long pause, drew an unsteady breath. "So, what about when it's all over? What then?"

"Lindsey…love."

And there it was, the pet name he'd been looking for. *Lindsey-love.* And now realized had been there all along, only he'd been too afraid to say it out loud. Why? he wondered. *Afraid it might be true?*

He took refuge in a tried and true cop-out. "It's not that simple."

She raised herself on one elbow and looked down at him, her bewitching eyes only smudges in the darkness. After what seemed an endless silence, she said very softly, "You think my father is guilty, don't you? And you think I'll blame you...hate you...for bringing him down."

"Lindsey..."

In a quick, almost violent movement, she sat up, pulled her knees to her chest and wrapped her arms around them. Her voice sounded breathless and muffled. "I wouldn't, you know. Even if he were guilty. Which I know he's not. But if he were, I wouldn't blame you." Her head swiveled toward him. "How could I? You're only doing your job. In fact, doing what I asked you to do. How could I blame *you?*"

He heard the anguish in her voice as she emphasized the last word and thought, *Yes, there it is.* "You would," he said gently, raising himself on one elbow. "Or maybe more than that, you'd blame yourself. Whichever way it goes, it's always going to be there between us."

Again, a flurry of movement in the darkness as she shook her head. "It doesn't have to be. People have overcome worse things. It's only an obstacle if you let it be. And maybe—"

He heard a sharp intake of breath, as if she'd stumbled, and when she continued there was a new note of breathlessness and pain in her voice.

Which was just what it was like, he thought—stumbling over the truth. Like stubbing your toe in the darkness.

"Maybe you *want* it to be. Because…maybe what you want is an excuse."

"An excuse?" he said. "For what?"

"An excuse not to try again." She paused, and he caught a furtive movement—her hand, brushing her cheeks. "Like me. I know what it's like, you know—to be so afraid of getting your heart broken, you won't let yourself take another chance."

Chapter 11

I had gone there to kill her—to finish the job I started. When I found she had no memory, and then they told me she was pregnant... How could I justify killing a child? And she didn't know me, didn't recognize me at all...

Excerpt from the confession of Alexi K.
FBI Files, Restricted Access,
Declassified 2010

Alan was a homicide cop; he was accustomed to listening to confessions. He knew not to interrupt with questions at this point, but simply to listen...and wait.

In the neutral, nonjudgmental darkness, Lindsey paused to gather her courage, and after a moment, went on.

"After my baby died, I had an operation—it's called a tubal ligation. I had my tubes tied, in other words. So I couldn't get pregnant again—ever. I couldn't stand to go through that again—the pain. I just couldn't. Other people seemed to be able to have miscarriages, lose babies, and try again and again. But not me." Her voice seemed to clog up, slow to a trickle, so she continued in a whisper. "It cost me my marriage…broke my parents' hearts." She paused once more, gathering strength. "And I've always convinced myself I was right to do what I did. But the truth is, I was just not brave enough. I was a coward, Alan. Afraid to take the chance." She made that surreptitious little movement again, brushing at tears. "Please…don't do what I did. Don't cut yourself off from relationships just because one didn't work out for you. Give—this—us—a chance."

What could he say to her? Lie to her? Make her promises he wasn't sure he could keep?

In the end he said nothing except to murmur her name, and gathered her into his arms even knowing that doing so may have been as much a lie as saying the words out loud. But to leave her to weep uncomforted seemed to him too great a cruelty. And besides, he needed the comfort as much as she did.

He made love to her again. It solved nothing, she knew—and she was fairly certain he knew that, too—but it felt so good, and for a short while, at least, it did make the pain go away. His hand between her thighs…his mouth on her breasts…his big body solid beneath hers, on top of hers… every place he touched her, every way he touched her—a little rough where her body craved roughness, gently, delicately, carefully where any but the lightest touch might have brought pain—gave such exquisite pleasure. There was no room for thought or feeling. He really did make the world go away—and at that moment, it was all she asked of him.

Then, like an uninvited guest, a line from another song, one neither of them had mentioned, popped into her mind. Something about raindrops blowing against windows, and then: *Make believe you love me...*

Longing sliced through her, sharp and bright and hot as a blade. She gasped; her body arched and opened to him, and he responded to her urgency as if he knew exactly what she needed. He drove himself into her, hard and deep, and her body clenched and tightened at first until he covered her mouth with his, claimed her with his mouth, his hands, his body...filled her completely, and drove everything else from her mind.

Much later, exhausted and hovering on the edge of sleep, she heard him groan, then whisper, *"Damn.* Forgot the condoms again."

She laughed, and fell headlong into oblivion.

"I keep coming back to it—the question Holt asked." Lindsey shook her head, then leaned it back against the headrest but didn't close her eyes. *"Why?"*

They were driving south on the 405 Freeway in light Sunday morning traffic. The storm had moved on east. Somewhere off to their right the Pacific was living up to its name, for once. On the left, distant mountains sported caps of new snow. The color palate was crisp and bright, the sky overhead a brilliant blue, dotted with artist's clouds. A chamber of commerce postcard day.

When Alan didn't reply, she looked over at him. His profile was sharp-edged, his eyes narrowed and focused on the road ahead. He was all cop this morning, and she was actually glad. It made it easier to put the night that had passed between them into its own compartment in her mind, something rare to be locked away…protected…kept separate from real life.

"I know you think my dad is guilty, that he's the one who kidnapped the McKinneys—" she still couldn't think of that young couple as her parents "—and shot them and threw them into the Chesapeake Bay…"

"Your mother says he did," Alan said quietly. "You want to believe she's confused, that she made a mistake. But she was right about everything else—having a different husband, a child named Jimmy, being shot, floating—why would she be confused about that one thing? The most important thing, maybe."

"But, *why?* It doesn't make sense. It seems pretty certain my dad was the man who showed up at the hospital and claimed Jane Doe as his wife, Sally Phillips. It's absolutely certain he's the man who raised me and made a happy home for me and my mother for the next forty years." Her voice was tight now, with the anger that constricted her throat and chest. "You tell me—how does it make any kind of sense that he's the same person who shot her in the first place?"

There was a long pause, and then Alan let out a slow, exasperated breath. "It doesn't. I know it doesn't." He threw her a quick, intense glance. "But, there *is* an answer to that question, and the only person who knows it is the man who calls himself Richard Merrill." His voice was hard, and she could see the muscles in his jaw clench. "I'm going to have to talk to him, Lindsey. You know that, don't you?"

She turned her head to look out the window and didn't reply.

Yes. I'm going to have to talk to him.

"But," Alan continued, "I need to have as much information as I possibly can before I do. The photos alone aren't enough. Which means I have to wait for everything from the Richmond PD, as well as Bob Faulkner's files—the Baltimore files on the McKinney case—to get here. He's sending them overnight, but because of the weekend they won't get here until at least Monday." He paused, then said, "Lindsey?" in a warning tone. And paused again. "He cannot know about this—do you understand me? You can't tell him what we know, or ask him about it yourself. In fact, you'd best stay completely away from him, if you don't think you can keep secrets from him. Okay?"

She couldn't seem to make herself utter a sound. She nodded, watching San Clemente slip past and the Pacific come into view beyond her window.

"Lindsey? Promise me you won't try to talk to him. Stay…away…from him. Got it?"

San Onofre nuclear power plant loomed ahead on the right, a giant pair of female breasts pointing at the sky. She stared at them with burning eyes. "Got it," she said.

Neither of them spoke again until they were pulling into Lindsey's driveway. Instead of dropping her off, Alan got out and walked her to her door, looking around him the way cops do, checking out the surroundings. One hand even went automatically to his right hip, she noticed, where his holster would be, if he'd had a weapon with him.

Remembering the last time we were here, she thought. *And Dad was here…coming down the driveway. My Dad. And now he's wishing for his gun?*

At her door, he took her face between his hands and looked into her eyes, and she thought for a moment he would kiss her. Instead, he said gravely, "Stay away from him, Lindsey. Please. There's no telling what he might do if he knows we're on to him."

"Dad would never hurt me," she said thickly.

She pulled away from him and put her key in the lock, opened the door and went inside. He didn't say anything more, or try to stop her. She closed the door, locked it, then leaned against it and let the tears come.

"I don't trust her," Alan said.

At the other end of the cell phone connection, Carl Taketa was silent for a moment. Then: "Do you really think she'd confront Merrill on her own?"

"She didn't promise she wouldn't," Alan said grimly. "And even if she did promise, I still wouldn't trust her. She's desperate for answers, and he's the only one who's got 'em. And, he's her daddy. She truly doesn't believe he'd harm her."

"Do you think he would?"

Alan let out a gusty breath. "Probably not. But that's not my only concern. The guy has changed identities before. He has financial resources. If he finds out we're on to him, we'll lose him for sure."

"You really think she'd tip him off?"

"Again—probably not. Not deliberately, anyway. But I have a feeling she's not a very good liar, not where he's concerned, and this is weighing heavily on her mind. She could easily say or do something that would make him suspicious. Look—you know I can't do anything until we get the DNA results showing a sibling relationship between Lindsey and Holt Kincaid. Without that there's no proof Karen McKinney and Susan Merrill are the same person, and even with DNA we can't definitively prove the Chesapeake Jane Doe is connected to either one."

"Come on," Carl said, "I don't think you'd have any trouble convincing a jury."

"Maybe not," Alan said, "which only makes Merrill

guilty of falsifying his identity. There's nothing to connect him to the shooting of Karen and James McKinney. The only way I'm going to get that is to sweat it out of him, and before I go after him I need more than what I've got now. Meanwhile, I don't want to take a chance on losing him. Partner, I hate like hell to ask you—I know it's Sunday, but he knows me, he knows my car—"

"Say no more. I'll sit on him until you can get the captain to assign surveillance."

"Alicia is going to hate me."

"Nah, that's the great thing about her being a cop, too. She'll understand."

"Well…thanks, pal. I owe you."

"What for? Giving me a piece of solving a forty-year-old murder? Shoot, man, I owe *you*."

Lindsey was stepping out of the shower when her cell phone rang. She grabbed a towel and picked up the phone with a shaking hand, knowing who it was before she even looked at the caller ID.

"Dad!" she said, as her chest and throat filled up with a lumpy mixture of guilt and grief.

"Lindsey? Where've you been, sweetheart? I've been trying to reach you for two days."

"Um…sorry about that." She tried to laugh, and it sounded like a cry of pain. "I…had my phone turned off most of the weekend. I was—Alan and I went to L.A."

"In all that rain? What in the world for?"

"We were…uh…we were visiting some friends of Alan's. Traffic was fine going in, but coming back it got pretty bad, so we stayed over and came on home this morning. I didn't think about calling. I'm sorry if you were worried, but there wasn't any reason to be."

"I know, I know, and you're an adult and don't need to check in with your old dad anymore, but…it wouldn't kill you to give me a call, would it? You're still my little girl, you know."

"I know…"

"Lindsey? What's the matter? Is something wrong?"

"No, no." Her eyes were shut tight. She struggled with all her strength to hold back tears…make her voice sound bright…normal. She forced a laugh, then sniffed and added, "I just got out of the shower, Dad. I'm dripping here."

"Oh! Well, for goodness' sake, don't catch cold. I won't keep you, honey. Just glad you're home safe."

"Me, too. Don't worry, I'm fine."

"I know you are. But I'll worry anyway. I love you, girlie." There was a pause, then: "Talked to your mother lately?"

"Not for a few days. I'm going to go see her tomorrow."

"Okay…well." There was the sound of an indrawn breath. "Tell her I love her, honey. Will you do that for me?"

"I will, Dad." She was holding her breath, afraid to breathe, afraid he would hear a sob in it. Her chest felt as though it would burst.

"Well…okay then. Guess I'll say g'night. Let you get dried off."

"'Night, Dad."

"I love you, honey."

"Love you, too…"

She broke the connection and turned blindly, first one way, then the other, in such agony she wanted nothing so much as to hurl the phone as far and as hard as she could. But of course she didn't. Instead she pressed the instrument against her forehead, closed her eyes and let the pent-up tears flow freely down her cheeks.

First thing Monday morning Alan knocked on Ron Tupman's door. The captain sounded surly, as usual, even that early on the first day of a new week, but he listened with his customary laser-like intensity while Alan filled him in on the weekend's developments in the Susan Merrill case.

"So," Tupman said when Alan had finished, "you're telling me Taketa's been sitting on Merrill's place all night?"

"Yes, sir, he has," Alan said. "Didn't want the man deciding to pull another disappearing act."

"So, you think his daughter—so-called—might tip him off?"

"I hope she won't, but…let's just say I'd rather not take that chance."

Tupman nodded and picked up his phone. "Well, let's get somebody out there to relieve Carl." He drilled Alan with a stare. "How long you figure before you'll have enough to bring him in?"

Alan considered. "Depends on what Richmond sends me. And the rest of the files from the Baltimore detective— Faulkner. Unless there's something there we all missed, I'm probably going to have to wait for the DNA."

Tupman nodded. "We'll take it a day at a time. Somebody'll be on him as long as needs to be."

"Thanks," Alan said, then added, knowing he probably didn't need to, "Unmarked cars—don't want to spook him."

Tupman glared at him and punched a button. "Got it," he said dryly.

* * *

Lindsey closed her mother's front door quietly behind her. Across the tiny apartment she could see her mother on the patio, snipping off spent blossoms from pots of chrysanthemums. It was a chilly, breezy day, and Lindsey was pleased to see she'd remembered to put on a sweater.

"Mom," she called, "it's me—Lindsey."

Susan looked up, and to Lindsey's relief, her expression changed from alarm and suspicion to a smile of recognition. "Oh—my goodness. Lindsey—how nice!" She waved her snippers at the array of pots on various tables and stands around the patio. "I was just cleaning up these mums—they're about done for the season, I think. I'm going to plant pansies next. Did you bring me some pansies?"

"I brought you pansies last week, Mom," Lindsey said, and hastened to add, as a look of uncertainty crossed her mother's face, "but I'll bring some more next time I come."

"Yellow ones," Susan said emphatically. "I like the yellow ones best. They brighten up the place. Well—" she pushed back her hair with the back of her hand, then pulled off her gloves and laid them and the snippers on the wrought-iron table "—shall we have something cold to drink? See what there is in the fridge. I think there might be some iced tea…"

Lindsey said, "Sounds good, Mom," and laid the manila envelope she'd brought with her on the table beside the gloves and snippers.

"What's this?"

Already on her way to the kitchen, Lindsey glanced back and said, "Just some pictures I brought to show you." She felt quivery inside, now that the moment was almost upon her. "Wait a minute, let me get us some tea first, okay?"

She opened the refrigerator, removed a flat of wilted pansies from the bottom shelf and put it on the counter next to the sink, then got two bottles of sweetened lemon-flavored tea and shut the door. She returned to the patio to find her mother staring blankly down at the sheet of paper in her hand. The manila envelope had fallen unnoticed to the floor.

"Mom?"

Susan put out a groping hand, and Lindsey lunged, reaching her in time to guide her into a chair. She pulled out a chair for herself and sat in it, facing her mother. The piece of paper, upon which was printed the copy of the wedding photograph of James and Karen McKinney, now rested on Susan's knees. Almost fearfully, Susan touched first one face, then the other.

"Do you recognize them?" Lindsey asked. Her throat hurt so intensely she could barely speak.

Susan's shaking fingertips caressed the groom's smooth cheek, almost as if it was warm flesh she felt instead of cold paper. She nodded, and a tear fell onto the image, making a small wrinkled circle. "James," she whispered. "Oh, James…" She looked up at Lindsey and her face was bathed in tears. "He's dead. That man killed him—the one who says he's my husband. He shot him. I asked him why, but he wouldn't answer me. Why? Why would anybody want to kill James? He was such a good, sweet, gentle man…"

Lindsey slid from her chair and, kneeling, gathered her mother into her arms. She held her mother while she cried and cried. And all the time, Susan just kept asking, *"Why?"*

* * *

On Monday afternoon, a packet of files arrived from the Richmond, Virginia, PD. Included in the file were several clear photos of the woman rescued from the Chesapeake Bay, the one that came to be called Chesapeake Jane Doe. Carl, being a bit more adept with computer stuff than Alan, scanned them into a facial recognition program along with the high school graduation portrait of Karen McKinney and a recent photo of Susan Merrill. Shortly thereafter the computer came up with a positive match: Jane Doe and Karen McKinney and Susan Merrill were one and the same.

"What do you think?" Carl asked as they stood together staring at the monitor screen. "Is this enough to pull him in?"

Alan nodded grimly. He had his cell phone in his hand and was punching in numbers.

"Calling Lindsey?"

Alan glanced at him as he listened to the rings. "I'd feel better knowing where she is and what she's doing before we do this. Don't want to take any chances on her getting into the middle of a situation."

Carl nodded.

After a moment, Alan put the phone back in his pocket and plucked his jacket off the back of his chair. "She's not answering. She might be out jogging—she leaves her phone home when she runs. I'm going to drive out there…see if I can locate her. We've got Merrill boxed in. Let's hold off on bringing him in until we've got his daughter under wraps."

Safe, he thought.

Lindsey left her car parked at the curb and walked up the driveway on legs that felt as if they might give way at any moment. The garage door was open, and so was the door to the backyard patio. She went on through, calling, "Dad?"

"Lindsey? I'm out here, honey—come on back."

He was cleaning the pool. How many times had she watched him do that? He was wearing a windbreaker with his Bermuda shorts and tennis sneakers with no socks—a typical San Diegan's concession to winter—standing with his legs a little apart to brace himself against the pull of the strainer, methodically moving it back and forth, back and forth... He could have installed an automatic cleaning system, like most of their friends had, especially now that they were all getting older, but he always insisted he liked the exercise.

"This is a nice surprise," he said, and as always his face had lit up at the sight of her. The smile almost instantly turned to a frown of concern as he got a better look at her face. "Honey? What's wrong? Has something happened?" As he spoke he was drawing the long-handled skimmer out of the water, laying it on the pool deck. He came toward her, drying his hands on his shorts, reaching for her. She backed away before he could touch her. His gaze dropped to the manila envelope in her hand, then rose again to her face. "Lindsey? What have you got there?"

She turned away from him and put the envelope on the patio table. She opened it and pulled out the wedding photo of Karen and James McKinney...slid it across the glass toward her father. When she looked up at him, she found that he was staring down at the photo, not looking at her.

"Where did you get this?" His voice sounded stifled.

"Do you recognize them, Dad?" She was amazed at how controlled her voice seemed.

He didn't reply. His face, his whole body seemed to have frozen.

Almost gently, she said, "You do, don't you?"

He cleared his throat. "Well, it's your mother, obviously, but I don't—did Alan give you this? Of course he did." He paused, and his smile was sad. "Is he even your boyfriend, Lindsey?"

She shook her head as if to clear away fog. "Maybe—I don't know—does it matter?" Her voice hardened. "You know him, don't you? Of course you do. How could you forget the face of the man you *killed?*"

He jerked as if she'd slapped him. "Lindsey? What are you talking about? Where did you get such an idea? I don't know what you—or Alan, the police, whoever—think I've done."

"No—don't lie to me." She was crying, suddenly. "The fact that I have that photo should tell you I know pretty much everything. The police do, too. The only thing they can't figure out—the thing I can't understand, no matter how hard I try, is *why?*"

There was a long silence. He drew a shaking hand over his face, which seemed to have aged a decade in a matter of minutes. "I have always known this day would come." His voice sounded oddly stilted, as if he were reading from something he'd written. He paused, then turned and started toward the house in a vague, lost sort of way. "I have something I must give you. Something I've been saving for you…"

"No!" Lindsey shouted at him, "Don't walk away. I want you to tell me why. Forty years of lies, pretending to be my father, saying you loved us—Mom and me—"

He turned back to her, his movements jerky, off-balance. "No—that was not pretense. I love you, Lindsey, as my own daughter. Your mother—I loved her, too. I think I loved her maybe from the first."

"Then why—how could you—"

"Please try to understand." He held out his hands to her in a kind of entreaty, but at the same time his voice seemed to grow stronger, to take on a note of determination—even pride. "I was a soldier. I was doing what I had been trained to do. It was my duty—my mission. I believed I was doing what I had to do—"

"You had to *kill* them?" She couldn't stop a shudder of revulsion.

"Yes!" His eyes were fierce; she'd never seen him look like that before. "They were the enemy—traitors to their country!" And just that quickly the fire died, and his face looked haggard and ravaged. "Or so I believed…"

He reached blindly for a chair and sat in it heavily, then raised tortured eyes to her face. "Please," he said hoarsely. "Sit down. I will tell you everything. But, you must let me begin at the beginning."

Chapter 12

*I thought it would be safer to have her close
to me. Then, I told myself, if her memory ever did
return, I would be able to deal with her. The years
went by and I dared to hope the day of reckoning
would never come.*

Excerpt from the confession of Alexi K.
FBI Files, Restricted Access,
Declassified 2010

Alan was standing on the steps of Lindsey's townhouse,
scowling at the top of a distant palm tree, the cell phone
pressed hard against his ear. "I'm at Lindsey's place," he
told Carl. "She's not here, and neither is her car."

"What're you thinking? She might have gone to confront
Merrill herself? Would she do that, knowing what we
know?"

"I don't know," Alan said, his voice reflecting the

darkness of his thoughts. "She might just have driven over to Mission Bay to take her run. Or...she might have decided to take matters into her own hands. I couldn't tell you. What's the surveillance on Merrill saying?"

"They haven't reported any movement, so I'm assuming he's staying put."

Alan let out an exasperated breath. "Yeah, but is he *alone?* What's the matter with those guys? Have to have everything spelled out?" He swore under his breath, making his way down the driveway in long strides to his car. "Find out, Carl. I want to know if Merrill's had any visitors."

"Gotcha," Carl said. "You heading over there?"

"On my way." He was already in his car. The engine fired and he drove through the gate and turned into the street with tires squealing.

"First, I should tell you that my name—the one I was given at birth—is Alexi Kovalenko. I was born in Kiev, which is the capital city of Ukraine."

This isn't happening, Lindsey thought. She fought desperately not to throw up. The words seemed to come at her in a fierce wind. She felt cold...almost paralyzed. And at the same time endangered...pursued. Like a nightmare in which she was chased endlessly while struggling to run on limbs weighed down with thick, deep mud. She prayed it was a nightmare, and that she would wake up and it would be over and quickly forgotten.

Though she tried not to, she must have made some sound because he—the stranger she'd called Dad for forty years—held up a hand asking, begging her to let him continue.

"Please...please listen. I am not a monster. What I did, I did for what I thought were very good reasons at the time..." He closed his eyes and put a hand over them—she saw this through a blur of tears—and after a moment, when she hadn't spoken or fled, he heaved in a careful breath and went on.

"At that time, of course, Ukraine was part of the U.S.S.R., and it was the era of Stalin. My father was a faithful member of the Party, so our family lived fairly well. Then came the war. Because of his connections, my father was able to have my mother and me sent away, to the east, to safety, so we escaped the terrible starvation and fighting that ravaged Ukraine for so many years. My father was killed during the battle for Kiev. Because he died a hero, my mother and I were well taken care of. After the war, when I was still a young boy, I was taken from my mother and sent to live in a different—very different—kind of village. I was told I had been selected for a special mission, a very rare opportunity to serve my country.

"Lindsey," he said, as she sat struggling to breathe… struggling to weep silently and not scream in anguished denial, "you are too young to remember how it was then, at the height of the Cold War. People on both sides lived in constant fear of nuclear holocaust, and the knowledge that there were thousands of warheads pointed at our cities and that anything—even a stupid mistake—could trigger annihilation. Both sides, understanding that knowledge was power, employed vast networks of spies and agents working to provide information as to what the other side was planning, what their capabilities were—well, I guess you've seen enough movies and read enough spy thrillers, that perhaps you have some idea—even if a romanticized one—what it was like."

He paused and looked at her as if waiting for her confirmation. No longer crying, she only stared back at him in numb silence, and after a moment he went on.

"Anyway—this 'village' where I was now to live was, in fact, a top secret project in this war for information. It had been constructed as an exact replica of a small town in the American Midwest, although it was located somewhere in the vast interior of the Soviet Union. There I lived and went to school—as an American boy. I learned to speak American English perfectly, without the slightest trace of an accent. In school I studied American history and government and literature. I ate American food, played American games, watched American movies, read American books. I became…American—but only on the outside. In my heart I remained a loyal Soviet citizen, completely dedicated to my country's cause.

"By the mid-1950s, when I was nearly twenty, I had completed my training and was considered ready to fulfill my mission. I, along with others who had completed the program—I have no idea how many of us there were—was smuggled into the United States, where I slipped seamlessly into American life. I had been provided with a background, all necessary documents. All I had to do was wait to be contacted and told what my mission was to be. In the meantime, I went to school, got a job, dated—but didn't marry. That would have made it too hard to keep my secret, I thought. And the years went by.

"Then, in the late summer of 1969, I received the orders I had been waiting for."

He paused for a long time, and Lindsey could feel him looking at her. When she didn't raise her eyes from her hands, clasped tightly together on the tabletop, once again he drew a breath and went on.

"I was to go to Baltimore, where I was to…*eliminate*—"

"Eliminate—you mean *kill*, don't you?"

He glanced at her, startled, perhaps, that she had finally spoken. "Yes—*kill*…two people. I was told these people were traitors to their country. Agents who had turned, gone over to the enemy."

"Traitors!" Her cry was one of pain, of outrage. "What are you talking about? He was a schoolteacher! She was a housewife—a mother. They weren't *spies!*"

A spasm of emotion twisted his face, before he lifted a hand to cover it. What the emotion was she didn't know or care—she had no desire to understand him, just then. "Yes…yes," he said in a ragged voice, "I know. But by the time I found that out, you see…it was already too late."

"You're not gonna like this," Carl said. His voice came through on Alan's Bluetooth, with too much background noise.

"Tell me," Alan said, eyes fixed grimly on the traffic ahead.

"The guys sitting on Merrill just informed me he has a visitor—arrived about forty-five minutes ago."

Alan swore. "And they're just telling us this *now?*"

"Guess they were told to report on Merrill's movements, so that's what they did. Anyway, from the description, sure sounds like Lindsey. Who else would it be?" There was a long, empty pause, while Alan fought back all sorts of emotions, none of them familiar to him, the most prominent of which was fear. Then Carl said, "What do you want me to do? Should I tell 'em to go in?"

"No. God, no. The last thing we want to do is provoke a hostage situation. No…just tell 'em to sit tight. I'm on my way."

His car was equipped with emergency lights and siren, which he didn't use often. He switched them both on now.

* * *

"I had no way of knowing," Richard—or Alexi—said. "Sometime between when I was told where to find my targets, and my arrival in Baltimore, they fled. And another young couple—innocents—moved into their apartment. How was I to know? They were the same approximate age...fit the general description..."

"They had a child!"

He hesitated, then seemed to steel himself. "That was unfortunate, but I didn't consider it important. After all, I'd been raised in a culture in which the bonds of family, even between parents and children, were considered less important than duty...loyalty to country. I had lived in America long enough to know the boy would be taken care of, perhaps even grow up stronger because of it. No, he wasn't a consideration to me at all." He waved a hand, then sat for a long moment gazing across the barrancas, disappearing now in the purple haze of sunset.

"Most of the rest...I think you probably already know. Everything was in place—the boat, the weights to take the bodies down..."

The bodies...my parents. Lindsey sat still, crying quietly. She felt empty.

"Everything went like clockwork. I waited...took them when they were away from home, and there were no witnesses. They seemed more bewildered than afraid..."

The words went on and on, falling on her ears like raindrops on windowpanes...she heard them, but they couldn't reach her.

I can't let them reach me. It would be unbearable, too terrible to imagine...to feel what it must have been like for them. To be taken, to know at last that they were going to die, and not to know why.

Oh, how she wished she could stop the words. Wished she could press Pause, then Rewind...go back to the day before she'd walked into the San Diego Police Department headquarters, back to before she'd met a homicide detective named Alan Cameron.

"When I saw the newspapers...when I knew she'd somehow survived, I went to the hospital. I went there to kill her, not only because she could identify me, but because it was my mission. I was a soldier, and I had to finish the task I had been ordered to do. But when she didn't know me at all...and I found out she was pregnant..." He lifted his hands, held them out in a gesture of entreaty. "What was I supposed to do? I couldn't justify killing a child. And then...I found out—my 'control,' the voice I only knew from the telephone, told me—I had made a terrible mistake and that she—they—weren't the people I was supposed to kill. So I ran. I cut my ties to my country, my duty. I took her away with me, and I prayed her memory would never come back. I grew to love her, and *you,* her child. You became *my* child. And for forty years I have tried to atone for what I did. I don't ask you to forgive me, Lindsey, only maybe to—"

"Forgive you?" Her voice was a whisper; she felt as though all the air had been sucked from her lungs. She recoiled from him, closing her eyes tightly, trying to shut out the images he'd imprinted on her brain.

So, she didn't see him go. Only heard the soft sigh of an exhalation, like a surrender.

"Okay, sweetheart," he said quietly, and it was her dad's voice again. "I understand."

She sat hunched in her chair with one arm pressed across her stomach, the other hand over her mouth, holding back howls of anguish, and listened to the patio door slide open.

Listened to footsteps crossing the tile kitchen floor. Heard the door to his office open...then close.

She didn't know what made her rise, cold with nameless fear, and dash into the house. Or how long it was after that—seconds...minutes—when she heard the gunshot.

Alan was pulling onto Merrill's street. He'd just reported his position and ETA to his partner when he heard Carl's radio, the sound coming through clearly on the hands-free cell phone transmission:

"Shots fired! Shots fired!"

Carl swore. "Did you—"

"I heard." Alan dropped the phone onto the seat and stepped on the gas.

He'd never been crazy about the so-called "adrenaline rush"—not like some thrill junkies he knew—but he was glad to have it kick in now. Knew it was what made him able to function as a police officer while on another level, one completely separate from the trained cop, he was just an ordinary man and more terrified than he'd ever been before in his life. Fear knotted his belly and hollowed his chest, but his hands were steady on the wheel as he aimed the car into the driveway of Richard Merrill's house, and screeched it to a halt. They were steady as he drew his weapon from its holster. He got out of the car and his voice was firm and clear as he shouted at the two uniforms who were dashing up the street toward him.

"How many shots?"

"Just heard the one,"

"Take the front—I'm going in the back."

He sprinted through the open garage, and he could hear the two officers pounding on the front door, shouting, "Police—open up!"

Then he was in the backyard, on the patio where such a short time ago he'd stood chatting with Richard Merrill while Chelsea played in the pool nearby. Now he crossed the open area in a half crouch, his weapon in a two-handed grip, every muscle, every nerve on full alert.

"Lindsey!" he yelled, and got no answer. "Richard Merrill—this is the police! Put down your weapon and come out of the house—now!"

He paused, frozen, but heard no sound. Cold to his core, he approached the open sliding glass door. There was no sound, no movement from within. From the other side of the house he could hear a thump and a crash as the front door was forced open, and he heard one of the uniforms yell again: "Police—put down your weapon!"

Alan crossed the dark kitchen and from a position beside the door, peered around it and down the hallway. Partway down, he saw light pouring from an open doorway. Merrill's study, if he remembered correctly. From the other direction he saw movement—the uniformed officers, advancing with guns drawn. He waved them back with a quick, emphatic motion.

"Lindsey?" he shouted again. "Lindsey, are you there? Are you all right?"

He heard nothing. The fear inside him grew...became a monster that threatened to overwhelm him. He fought it down. Breathed deeply...in...out. And then, on legs he no longer felt, he moved slowly, steadily toward that open doorway. Moving in a nightmare, feeling nothing else but dread, he flattened himself against the wall, his weapon pointing at the ceiling. *Lindsey*...he prayed silently, and looked around the door frame, into the room.

And this time he said it aloud, on a rush of anguished breath. "Oh, God...Lindsey..."

She was sitting on the floor, where Richard Merrill lay sprawled on the patterned rug beside his desk. Merrill's head was in her lap. There was blood on the rug and on her hands and her clothes, even a smear on her cheek where she'd wiped it. A manila envelope lay on the desktop. A small handgun, a revolver—looked like a .38 caliber—lay on the rug near the body. For that's what it clearly was.

Hearing Alan's voice, she lifted her eyes to stare at him, her beautiful eyes glittering like jewels in her marble-white face. And she spoke in a voice that was clogged with tears but strong and fierce nonetheless.

"He would never have hurt me," she said.

It was later, Alan didn't know exactly how much. He'd become so engrossed in the typewritten document he'd been reading that he'd lost track of time.

He was leaning against the fender of his car, reading by the light of the floodlamps that had been set up in the street in front of the Merrill house. Crime scene tape surrounded the house and blocked off access to the street except to residents and authorized personnel. On the other side of the tape, neighbors still stood around in small clusters, some talking quietly with each other, others just standing… watching. There wasn't much to see. Inside the house, a forensics team had been going about its business, and would be doing so for quite some time, probably. The medical examiner had come and gone, taking with him the zipper-bagged body of Richard Merrill.

Or more accurately, Alan thought, staring down at the document in his hands, Alexi Kovalenko.

Carl Taketa was coming down the driveway toward him. Alan straightened and picked up the transparent evidence bag that lay on the hood of his car. Inside the bag was a manila envelope that still bore along its edges traces of the masking tape that had once presumably held it stuck securely to the bottom of Richard Merrill's middle desk drawer.

"Here you go," Carl said, and handed him a single sheet of paper, similar to the ones Alan held in his hands. "The CSI guys were cool about it—turned their backs and pretended they didn't see me using the copy machine."

"Thanks," Alan said. He put the sheet of paper with the others. The last page. He slid the entire document into the manila envelope, closed it, then closed and sealed the evidence bag. He put the bag back on the hood of the car and looked up at Carl. "You got the—"

"Right here." Carl took a folded sheet of paper out of his shirt pocket and gave it to Alan. Alan took it and put it in his own pocket.

Alan nodded toward the place where an ambulance was parked next to the curb a little farther down the street. He could see Lindsey sitting in the open back of the ambulance, talking to a paramedic, a blanket wrapped around her shoulders. He hadn't had a chance to talk to her since Carl and the lab and medical crews had arrived, having removed himself from the investigation due to his own personal involvement in the case.

"How is she?" he asked Carl now, keeping his tone carefully impersonal.

Carl, understanding, did the same. "She's okay. Negative for gun shot residue—looks like a pretty straightforward case of suicide. They've been treating her for shock." He paused, let out a breath. "Small wonder."

Alan picked up the evidence bag. "You get a chance to read this?"

Carl shook his head. "Just the first part. Wish I could

have read more of it. I have an idea once the Feebs take custody of this case, that's the last anybody's going to see of that document for a while." He paused, then added, "Helluva thing, huh?

"Yeah," Alan said.

"Wonder why he did it—writing everything down like that. You know?"

"He did it for *her,*" Alan said heavily. "He hoped she'd never have to read it. But if it ever came out—the truth—he wanted her to understand."

"How many others do you suppose there are—people like Merrill? My God—back in the fifties and sixties, there was all this paranoia about 'spies among us'—wild tales, I always thought. Now, turns out it was true." He shook his head again, in a kind of wonderment. "Didn't anybody ever think about what happened to all those spies when the country and the cause they worked for suddenly ceased to exist?"

Alan snorted softly. "Well, I guess we know what happened to one of 'em."

Carl stared at the house, where the people responsible for sorting out tragedies and assigning blame and responsibility for them were still going about their business. "What were they supposed to do? Pack up and go home?" He looked back at Alan. "Except...home wasn't *there* anymore. It's *here.*"

Alan didn't say anything, and they stood together in the night, under the floodlights, gazing at the activity all around them. Then Carl said without turning, "They're probably about done with her. Why don't you take her home?"

Alan looked at his partner. He felt tired, suddenly, more tired than he'd ever felt in his life, that he could remember.

And at the same time, oddly *wired,* as if there was a low-voltage current running just under his skin.

Carl took the evidence bag with the manila envelope from Alan's hand. "Go on," he said. "I got this covered. No need for you to stick around tonight."

Alan watched him walk back up the driveway toward the house. After a moment he took the folded piece of paper out of his pocket, unfolded it, read what was written there, then folded it again and put it back in his pocket. Then he straightened up and walked down the driveway, down the sidewalk to where Lindsey was.

Alan unlocked her door for her, then stepped in and took a quick look around before standing aside to let her go in ahead of him. He always did that. Force of habit, Lindsey thought; he probably wasn't even aware he was doing it.

She walked slowly across the tiled entry and stepped into her living room, which always before had given her a sense of warmth and welcome. Now the room seemed only vaguely familiar to her, like a room in a house she'd maybe visited once or twice. Feeling desperately weary, she turned to look at Alan, who had closed the door behind him and dropped the key onto the table in the entry, and stood now, watching her, hands in his trouser pockets.

"You're not going to leave me alone, are you?" she asked, smiling a little.

"Not unless you want me to," he said gravely.

She snorted, and after a moment said, "Well, I'm not about to beg."

"You don't have to beg," he said. "Obviously. I'm here, aren't I?"

"Yeah, you're here—or rather...*there.* Which is fine, if that's where you want to be, because like I said, I'm not going to—" As she was rattling on he was moving toward her, and before she could finish he'd gathered her into his arms, and her world once again became a warm and safe place.

He smelled so good…so clean. After a while she expelled a sigh against his shirtfront and murmured, "You must think me terribly needy."

"I don't."

"Hmm…right." She pushed away from him and looked down at the jacket someone—one of the EMTs, maybe—had given her to put on over her blood-stained clothes. It was way too big and covered the worst of it, even on her pants. She'd washed her hands after they'd tested her for gunshot residue, but she still felt sticky. And the smell… She touched her nose with the back of her hand and gazed around at nothing as she fought back a wave of nausea. "Um…can I get you anything? Some coffee?"

"You don't need to wait on me," he said.

She knew, without looking at him, that his eyes would have the softness that had first appealed to her when he'd spoken so gently to her mother. But it wasn't the kind of softness she wanted now.

"Yes," she snapped, "I do." While she talked she was moving again, just…moving, barely knowing where. Then she was in the kitchen, closing the curtains across the glass patio doors, opening cupboards, closing them again.

She felt his hands on her arms, turning her. He pulled out one of the stools beside the counter and sat on it, then drew her onto his lap.

"I need to do…something," she said.

"Yes, you do," he said, "but there are better things."

"Like what? Oh—I guess I should take a shower," she said, answering her own question.

"That's one," Alan said, nodding.

"I knew it—I stink."

"You don't."

"Liar." She'd stiffened, and was trying to get off his lap, but he only settled her more closely against him, one hand coming to guide her head firmly into the curve of his neck and shoulder.

"You don't stink," he said, "but if you did, I wouldn't care."

She went still, and for a long time lay against him listening to the sound of his heartbeat and the words he'd spoken. They seemed to rumble around in her head like some sort of distant and continuous thunder. Finally, she lifted her head so she could look at his face, and said, "Wow. That's...wow."

She touched his cheek...laid her hand along the side of his face, feeling the prickle of his beard against her palm. His eyes gazed steadily back at her. She stroked her thumb across his lips, and they parted slightly. A shiver ran through her, and, to her wonderment, through him, too.

"I thought you said this was a bad idea," she whispered.

His lips curved in a wry smile. "It's growing on me."

Laughter...pleasure...two things she'd thought she'd never experience again...bubbled deep inside her. She stirred a little and said with a tiny hiccup of laughter, "That's not all that's growing."

A chuckle shook his chest. "I know. What can I say?" He kissed her forehead and drew her head back down onto his shoulder. Then he said huskily, "But this isn't about sex. I can just hold you all night long, if that's what you want."

She slipped off his lap and turned to look at him. "I

would be very disappointed if you did that," she said gravely.

He unfolded himself and rose slowly from the stool. "Why is that?"

"What do you mean, *Why?* Because I would very much like you to make love to me. But like I said, I won't b—"

He took her face between his hands and kissed her, stopping the words in her mouth.

He'd kissed her before, but this was different. She knew it…felt it. She felt weak and shaky inside, and gripped his wrists and held on to them for support. When he lifted his head at last, she stood for a long moment with her eyes closed, then whispered, "But first…a shower."

"I've got no problem with that," he said, smiling.

Later, lying naked and spent beside him, Lindsey said, "I wouldn't—I don't—blame you. Or hold it against you. But I do blame myself. You were right about that."

His hand didn't stop stroking her back. "Why?"

"He asked me to forgive him, but I was in such shock…I couldn't look at him. I shrank from him, Alan. And that's when he…when he…"

"For what it's worth, I believe he did the only thing he could."

She rose up and stared at him, and he touched her cheek and then went on. "He'd lost everything, love. Everything that mattered. You…your mother. The rest didn't mean much."

She closed her eyes and swallowed, then said thickly, "He was wrong, you know. He hadn't lost me. I think I would have forgiven him. I *have* forgiven him. Maybe that's crazy, but no matter what he did, he was my dad. He loved me. Nothing can ever change that."

"No," Alan said. "Not crazy."

She lay quietly in his arms for a while, then raised herself again on one elbow to look down at him. "I want you to know," she said, in a voice that shook only a little, "that this isn't all about needing you to help me make it through the night."

"No? What is it, then?" Was he daring her? His smile seemed…tender.

Steeling herself one last time, she took a deep breath, and stepped out of the shadows and into the light. And felt more naked…exposed…vulnerable than any time before in her life.

"It's about me loving you," she said solemnly, "and offering you sex so that you will stay with me and grow to love me back."

His smile widened briefly, then vanished, to be replaced by an expression more appropriate for a priest hearing someone's most sacred secrets. He cleared his throat. "Uh…not that I don't appreciate the sex—am pretty happy about it, in fact—but it's not necessary in order for me to stay with you. Or love you back."

She looked at him for a long time. Then, whispering, "For real?"

"Yeah," he said in a raspy voice. "For real."

"What changed your mind?"

"About loving you? Nothing. I started doing that quite a while ago. But about giving us a chance…well, *you* did for starters." His smile flickered. "I didn't much like being called a coward. But what really did it, was…well, just a minute."

He shifted her and sat up. She watched him, her head propped on her hand, as he walked naked across the room to where he'd left his clothes, hung over the back of a chair.

He took something from the pocket of his shirt—a folded piece of paper. He came back, sat on the edge of the bed and handed the paper to her. His eyes seemed uncommonly bright.

Tears? she thought. *No. Impossible. This is Alan. Tough, hardened, homicide cop. It can't be tears.*

"This is the last page of Alexi Kovalenko's confession—I had Carl make me a copy." His voice was rough; he paused to clear his throat. "I think he meant it for you. I guess you could say they're his last words."

Lindsey looked at him in wonderment, half in fear. Then she took the paper from him, unfolded it, and through a shimmer of her own tears, read what was written there:

> *I could never understand why she survived.*
> *Of course, I did not believe in God, then.*
> *Later, I came to believe He had given both of us*
> *a second chance.*

She looked up at him, smiled radiantly and whispered, "Yes. Oh, yes."

Epilogue

San Diego, California
Thanksgiving Day

Holt Kincaid paused on the doorstep of the one-story, Spanish-style apartment. He turned to Brenna, who was holding their son, Jamie.

"You do know, she probably won't have any idea who I am."

"I know," Brenna said. "But that's okay. *You* know."

She smiled at him and briefly leaned her head against his shoulder. Jamie reached out his fat baby hand and patted his face and whispered, "Dah."

Holt took one more breath and knocked. Lindsey opened the door. Her face seemed flushed, and her eyes were brilliant. Behind her, he could see Alan, just hovering, one hand on her shoulder. Protecting her. Holt liked that.

"Hi—come in," Lindsey said, sounding slightly out of breath.

Holt moved past her, into a small living room, and Brenna followed him. "Smells fantastic," he said.

"Hope you're hungry," Lindsey said. "Turkey's about done—there's enough food for an army."

"Wouldn't be Thanksgiving," Holt said. "Where…is she—"

And then Alan was there, and on his arm, as if he were escorting a princess, a tall, slender woman wearing an apron over her blouse and slacks. Her salt-and-pepper hair was worn in an old-fashioned pageboy style. Her smile was brilliant but uncertain.

"Mom," Lindsey said, taking her mother's hand, "company's here."

Gamely, like a little girl remembering her manners, Karen McKinney smiled and held out her hand, first to Brenna. "Hello—do I know you? Who is this?" She touched Jamie's cheek. "Such a pretty baby." Her eyes moved on…found Holt's face. She seemed to stagger. Her hands rose, shaking, to her face, and her eyes widened and filled with tears.

"James," she whispered. And then, as the tears rolled down her cheeks: "Oh, James, where have you been? I thought you were dead. I've missed you so!"

Holt looked at Lindsey, who gave him a shrug and an apologetic smile. He wasn't sure what to do. Thinking he ought to just go along with the fact that his mother had obviously mistaken him for her husband, he took his son from Brenna's arms and said, "This is Jamie."

To his surprise, Karen laughed. "Silly, it's Jimmy, not Jamie! Think I don't know my own sweet boy?" She held out her arms, and, still not sure what to do, Holt handed his son over to his grandmother. Jamie promptly wriggled, demanding to be put down.

"Tell her," Lindsey said quietly. "Go ahead and tell her the truth. Tell her this child isn't her Jimmy, but her grandson, and that *you* are Jimmy, all grown up. She may not understand completely…but then again, I think she just might."

Holt hesitated. His mother, straightening up after setting her grandson down, gazed at him in bewilderment. He took her hands in both of his…feeling her hands for the first time in forty years, and yet…he felt as though he knew their touch. He lifted a hand and gently brushed away a tear from his mother's cheek.

"Hello, Mama," he said huskily, smiling through tears. "It's me…Jimmy. I've missed you, too."

* * * * *

Harlequin offers a romance for every mood!
See below for a sneak peek from
our suspense romance line
Silhouette® Romantic Suspense.
Introducing HER HERO IN HIDING by
New York Times *bestselling author Rachel Lee.*

Kay Young returned to woozy consciousness to find that she was lying on a soft sofa beneath a heap of quilts near a cheerfully burning fire. When she tried to move, however, everything hurt, and she groaned.

At once she heard a sound, then a stranger with a hard, harsh face was squatting beside her. "Shh," he said softly. "You're safe here. I promise."

"I have to go," she said weakly, struggling against pain. "He'll find me. He can't find me."

"Easy, lady," he said quietly. "You're hurt. No one's going to find you here."

"He will," she said desperately, terror clutching at her insides. "He always finds me!"

"Easy," he said again. "There's a blizzard outside. No one's getting here tonight, not even the doctor. I know, because I tried."

"Doctor? I don't need a doctor! I've got to get away."

"There's nowhere to go tonight," he said levelly. "And if I thought you could stand, I'd take you to a window and show you."

But even as she tried once more to pull away the quilts, she remembered something else: this man had been gentle when he'd found her beside the road, even when she had kicked and clawed. He hadn't hurt her.

Terror receded just a bit. She looked at him and detected signs of true concern there.

The terror eased another notch and she let her head sag on the pillow. "He always finds me," she whispered.

"Not here. Not tonight. That much I can guarantee."

Will Kay's mysterious rescuer protect her
from her worst fears?
Find out in HER HERO IN HIDING
by New York Times *bestselling author Rachel Lee.*
Available June 2010, only from
Silhouette® Romantic Suspense.

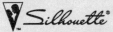

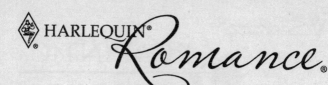

Four friends, four dream weddings!

On a girly weekend in Las Vegas, best friends Alex, Molly,
Serena and Jayne are supposed to just have fun and forget
men, but they end up meeting their perfect matches!
Will the love they find in Vegas stay in Vegas?

Find out in this sassy, fun and wildly romantic miniseries
all about love and friendship!

Saving Cinderella! by MYRNA MACKENZIE
Available June

Vegas Pregnancy Surprise by SHIRLEY JUMP
Available July

Inconveniently Wed! by JACKIE BRAUN
Available August

Wedding Date with the Best Man
by MELISSA McCLONE
Available September

www.eHarlequin.com

HRI7663

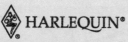

The Best Man in Texas
TANYA MICHAELS

Brooke Nichols—soon to be Brooke Baker—
hates surprises. Growing up in an unstable
environment, she's happy to be putting down
roots with her safe, steady fiancé. Then she meets
his best friend, Jake McBride, a firefighter and
former soldier who's raw, unpredictable and
passionate. With his spontaneous streak and
dangerous career, Jake is everything Brooke is
trying to avoid…so why is it so hard to resist him?

Available June
wherever books are sold.

"LOVE, HOME & HAPPINESS"

REQUEST YOUR FREE BOOKS!

2 FREE NOVELS PLUS 2 FREE GIFTS!

ROMANTIC SUSPENSE

Sparked by Danger, Fueled by Passion.

YES! Please send me 2 FREE Silhouette® Romantic Suspense novels and my 2 FREE gifts (gifts are worth about $10). After receiving them, if I don't wish to receive any more books, I can return the shipping statement marked "cancel." If I don't cancel, I will receive 4 brand-new novels every month and be billed just $4.24 per book in the U.S. or $4.99 per book in Canada. That's a saving of 15% off the cover price! It's quite a bargain! Shipping and handling is just 50¢ per book.* I understand that accepting the 2 free books and gifts places me under no obligation to buy anything. I can always return a shipment and cancel at any time. Even if I never buy another book from Silhouette, the two free books and gifts are mine to keep forever.

240/340 SDN E5Q4

Name	(PLEASE PRINT)	
Address		Apt. #
City	State/Prov.	Zip/Postal Code

Signature (if under 18, a parent or guardian must sign)

Mail to the Silhouette Reader Service:
IN U.S.A.: P.O. Box 1867, Buffalo, NY 14240-1867
IN CANADA: P.O. Box 609, Fort Erie, Ontario L2A 5X3

Not valid for current subscribers to Silhouette Romantic Suspense books.

Want to try two free books from another line?
Call 1-800-873-8635 or visit www.morefreebooks.com.

* Terms and prices subject to change without notice. Prices do not include applicable taxes. N.Y. residents add applicable sales tax. Canadian residents will be charged applicable provincial taxes and GST. Offer not valid in Quebec. This offer is limited to one order per household. All orders subject to approval. Credit or debit balances in a customer's account(s) may be offset by any other outstanding balance owed by or to the customer. Please allow 4 to 6 weeks for delivery. Offer available while quantities last.

Your Privacy: Silhouette is committed to protecting your privacy. Our Privacy Policy is available online at www.eHarlequin.com or upon request from the Reader Service. From time to time we make our lists of customers available to reputable third parties who may have a product or service of interest to you. If you would prefer we not share your name and address, please check here. ☐

Help us get it right—We strive for accurate, respectful and relevant communications. To clarify or modify your communication preferences, visit us at www.ReaderService.com/consumerschoice.

SRS10R